. C.   ssful

atha   well

a quartet of]   featur-

; heroine Lady Rose tem before the latest of Regency

mance series and a stand-alone murder mystery,

Skeleton in the Closet – all published by Constable

Robinson. She left a full-time career in journalism

urn to writing, and now divides her time between

Cotswolds and Paris. Visit www.agatharaisin.com

more, or follow M. C. Beaton on Twitter:

1c_beaton.

The Waverley Women series by M. C. Beaton

The First Rebellion
Silken Bonds
The Love Match

The First Rebellion

M. C. Beaton

Constable • London

CONSTABLE

First published by Crest, 1989

First electronic edition published 2011
by RosettaBooks LLC, New York

This edition first published in Great Britain in 2014 by Constable

3 5 7 9 10 8 6 4 2

Copyright © M. C. Beaton, 1989, 2011, 2014

The moral right of the author has been asserted.

A CIP catalogue record for this book
is available from the British Library.

ISBN: 978-1-47211-432-7 (A-format paperback)
ISBN 978-1-47210-155-6 (ebook)

Typeset in Berthold Baskerville by TW Typesetting, Plymouth, Devon
Printed and bound by CPI Group (UK) Ltd, Croydon, CR0 4YY

Constable
is an imprint of
Constable & Robinson Ltd
100 Victoria Embankment
London EC4Y 0DY

ONE

London had come to life again. Fuddled with wine and sick with fatigue, gamblers reeled from the clubs in St James's in the early morning hours. Tall houses blazed with lights as rout followed ridotto and ridotto followed musicale. There were fêtes champêtres in the Surrey fields and wicked nights at Vauxhall Gardens, where the women of cracked reputation haunted the Dark Walk to entice the drunken dandies. Ladies who had been refused vouchers to Almack's Assembly Rooms in King Street screamed and fainted and threatened suicide. Mothers of hopeful daughters gossiped and intrigued. The daughters practiced the art of flirting and dancing, and declared themselves to be dying of love for everyone and anyone. They lisped in baby voices, wore fluttering, nearly transparent muslin, spoke bad French, and lived in dread of the day when they might have to return to the country, unwed or unspoken for.

The London Season had begun.

But in the midst of all this hectic atmosphere of gossip and speculation, vice and intrigue, stood one calm and elegant house, its very atmosphere aloof from the squabbles of the marriage market.

The house stood in Hanover Square. Few were particularly interested in the doings of its inhabitants, and a few thought it must be a seminary for young ladies. For every day at three o'clock the front door was opened and out stepped a stout lady followed by three misses, all dressed the same and all with their hair braided under their drab hats.

They would walk slowly ten times around the square and then disappear indoors again. They had become such a common sight that hardly anyone wondered at the regularity of this strange promenade.

Except Lady Artemis Verity.

Lady Artemis was a widow who lived on the opposite side of the square. She was still young, frivolous, malicious, and on the lookout for a handsome husband. She was often bored and spent most of her afternoons lying on a chaise longue at the window of her drawing room, which overlooked the square. She could not be bothered reading or sewing or painting or playing the piano. She only came to life after dark when she could don one of the latest creations and star at a ball or party. She was accounted pretty, having glossy brown hair, a skin unpitted by smallpox, all her teeth, a shapely if plump figure, well-rounded arms, and a neat ankle.

One day she was lying on her chaise longue as usual, thinking about as little as it is possible for the human mind to think, when out of the corner of her half-closed eyes, she saw the little procession emerge.

For the first time she watched the lady and the three girls with more than idle curiosity. It could not be a seminary surely, not with only three young misses. It was hard to tell what the girls looked like, for each wore a hat the shape of a coal scuttle and in any case, from her vantage point, she could only see the tops of their heads.

She rang the bell and when a footman answered, she ordered him to find out the identity of the lady with the three girls who lived across the square.

After a short time the footman returned. He said the occupant of the house was a Mrs Waverley, a widow, and the three girls were her daughters. The footman said he knew one of the maids who worked for Mrs Waverley and she had told him that there were no menservants in the house. Mrs Waverley despised men and espoused the cause of rights for women.

'A bluestocking,' murmured Lady Artemis. 'How terribly boring,' and put the matter out of her mind.

That was until that very evening when she attended Almack's and found that the Earl of Tredair had come to Town. Lord Tredair was tall, rich, and handsome. He was in his thirties and unwed, and looked every bit as bored as Lady Artemis often felt.

3

The assemblies at Almack's were confined to Wednesday nights during the Season. 'Selection with a vengeance, the very quintessence of aristocracy. Three fourths of the nobility knocked in vain for admission. Into this sanctum sanctorum, of course, the sons of commerce never think of entering on the sacred Wednesday evening,' wrote Captain Gronow. If dancing was the ostensible object of Almack's existence, the place was useful in other ways. It formed a sort of matrimonial bazaar and its tables, spread with tepid lemonade, weak tea, tasteless orgeat, stale cakes, and thin slices of bread and butter, were often the scenes of tender proposals.

Lady Artemis attended Almack's every Wednesday in the hope of finding a new husband. She was twenty-five, but was sure she looked nineteen. She had plenty of courtiers and had more or less decided to settle for one of them, until she saw the Earl of Tredair and immediately knew that no one else would do. He was tall with thick black hair, a thin, clever, high-nosed face, and eyes of a peculiar green, like sea-washed glass. He had a supple athlete's body and his legs were finer than Gentleman Jackson's. But it was his air of lazy sensuality that quickened Lady Artemis's pulse.

She pretended to lose her footing while passing him en route to the refreshment room and clutched at him for support and then blushed and begged his pardon. Lady Artemis was very accomplished by the standards of the Regency. She could blush and cry at will.

'I am sure the fault was mine,' said Lord Tredair calmly. 'Allow me to fetch you something. A glass of lemonade?'

'Thank you, Lord Tredair,' said Lady Artemis demurely. 'But I shall accompany you, or some of my tiresome beaux will continue to bore me with their proposals of marriage.'

The interest in his eyes faded and his face became a polite mask of boredom. But he presented her with a glass of lemonade, found her a chair, and then stood beside her. Lady Artemis could sense he was poised for flight and wondered how to catch his interest.

'Are you enjoying the Season?' she asked.

'No, I am not,' he said. 'I feel I made a mistake in leaving the country.'

Lady Artemis was sophisticated and quick enough to know that he had suddenly lost interest in her and was trying to get rid of her. She wanted to attract him and felt at a loss. Usually her beauty was enough to keep any man glued to her side.

She said boldly, 'I am not used to gentlemen finding me tiresome.'

A certain flash of insolence crossed those odd eyes of his as he looked down at her. 'You must think me a sad fellow,' he said. 'I doubt if any man in his right mind could find anyone so fair, tiresome. You are not drinking your lemonade,' he added in tones that obviously meant, 'Pray drink it so that I may leave.'

The dancers were being urged to take their partners for a waltz. Lady Artemis knew her partner would be searching for her, but longed to dance with

5

the earl. She fluttered her fan and sighed, 'I do so adore the waltz.'

'Then you are fortunate,' said the earl with a sudden charming smile, 'for if I am not mistaken, your partner is approaching now.'

Lady Artemis looked up and sure enough her partner, Captain Ian Finlay, was bowing before her. She rose gracefully and curtsied to the earl and moved off on the arm of the captain.

The earl was joined by his friend, the Honorable John Fordyce. 'You are a lucky man,' said Mr Fordyce. 'I wish Lady Artemis would look on me with such favor.'

'Is that her name?' said the earl. 'Vastly pretty, but nothing out of the way.'

Mr Fordyce looked at his friend with affectionate amusement. The earl attended each Season for a few weeks, but quickly became bored and retreated to the country. He often said he had decided to get married, but usually he contented himself by having a brief affair with some comet from the opera.

'Is there nothing society can offer you to keep you in town this time?' pursued Mr Fordyce.

'I should not think so,' said the earl. 'It is always the same, you know, balls and routs and silly misses. They are all so well trained that they all sound the same. I despair of finding anyone different or out of the ordinary. In any case, you, too, are fated to remain a bachelor, for you always pursue exactly the sort of female who is bound to turn you down.'

Mr Fordyce smiled. He was a small man with neat

features and a trim figure. He was of good family, but his income from estates in Sussex was small. He always fell in love with the reigning belle of the Season and was always refused, which was why he, too, was still unwed.

'On the other hand,' the earl went on ruefully, 'there was no need for me to be quite so rude to Lady Artemis. I shall attempt to talk to her before I leave and be as charming as possible.'

'I do not know why you consider being pleasant to Lady Artemis such an effort,' said Mr Fordyce, turning to watch the dancers through the open door of the refreshment room. He had a clear view of Lady Artemis. Under a delicate tiara of gold and garnets – diamonds were out of fashion – her glossy brown curls shone in the candlelight. She moved with grace, the thin, fine muslin of her gown fluttering about her body.

'Perhaps I shall become a crusty old recluse,' said Lord Tredair. 'Striding about my estates and running for cover anytime I see guests arriving.'

Lord Tredair did not expect Lady Artemis would be so bold as to seek him out again. But no sooner was the waltz over than she appeared in the refreshment room and came straight up to him as if they were old friends. 'You are still here, my lord,' she cried. 'You do not dance.'

'Perhaps later,' said the earl.

'It is so very hot, and I am so very tired,' said Lady Artemis. 'But all the chairs seem to have been taken. Oh, there is a sofa against the wall over there.'

The earl bowed and escorted her to the sofa and after a little hesitation sat down beside her.

'Have you seen the new opera by Mr Kenny?' asked Lady Artemis. 'It is called, *Oh! This Love!*'

'No, I am afraid not.'

'It has an ingenious plot. The Count Florimond, during a runaway expedition in his youth, conceives an invincible passion for the Countess Belflora, who, to indulge a romantic fancy, had at that time assumed the character and dress of a peasant girl.'

'I may not have seen it,' interrupted the earl, 'but from your description of the plot, I swear I must have seen a dozen like it.'

'Oh, there is no pleasing you, you horrible man,' said Lady Artemis, rapping him playfully with her fan. 'I declare, I think you are a secret Methodist or one of those gentlemen who find us social butterflies tiresome and prefer the company of bluestockings, the sort of women who despise men and talk of their rights from morning till night.'

'I might be interested if I ever met a genuine one,' said the earl. 'But they are usually women who are unmarriageable and want an excuse to take their disappointment and spleen out on the world.'

'How hard you are! How bitter! And yet across from where I live in Hanover Square, there dwells a widow who appears to be the genuine article, for she has three daughters, no menservants, and lives like a recluse.'

'Indeed!' The earl looked at Lady Artemis with interest. 'And do you know this lady?'

Lady Artemis thought quickly. If she said, no, he would lose interest in her again. So she said, 'I have the pleasure of her acquaintance.'

'I cannot believe that a widow with three daughters can be uninterested in the world of men,' said the earl.

'But that is the case, I assure you,' said Lady Artemis eagerly. 'Should you wish an introduction, I could arrange it.'

'I'll wager you a hundred guineas the woman is a fraud,' said the earl.

Lady Artemis smiled. 'I accept your wager,' she said triumphantly, knowing that the bet forged a certain intimacy between them. 'You shall hear from me very shortly.'

She rose and curtsied and left him, knowing that if she stayed longer with him, he would lose interest again. She had a feeling of exhilaration. Catching Lord Tredair was like playing a salmon. The bait, the line, the hook, the tug, the final pull, and she would have him gasping at her feet.

It was only then that she realized she would have to ingratiate herself into Mrs Waverley's household.

Fanny Waverley pulled on her gloves two days later and stood by the window, waiting for the summons to go downstairs for the annual promenade. She thought it might be possible to die from boredom.

Outside, stretched the Germanic facade of the buildings of Hanover Square, four-story houses built of dark gray, red, and yellow stock brick. It was one of

9

the best addresses in London and Fanny wondered, not for the first time, what point there was in living at a fashionable address if one was determined not to be fashionable.

Fanny, like her 'sisters,' Frederica and Felicity, were not related and had all been taken from an orphanage and adopted by Mrs Waverley.

Mrs Waverley had told the girls that she had rescued them in order to bring them up as her disciples. They must spread the word about women's rights. They must encourage poor, oppressed women to rise up.

Fanny had been fourteen when they had been adopted by Mrs Waverley and given her name. She could often remember the elation at being taken out of the dark and freezing orphanage on a foggy winter day and moved into warmth and light and luxury in Hanover Square.

But Fanny was now nineteen. Fanny did not like either Frederica or Felicity for the simple reason that Mrs Waverley had operated on a divide-and-rule policy from the start, cleverly setting one girl against the other so that she herself could reign supreme in each one's affections.

Also Fanny was tired of being dressed up as a little girl every time they went out of the house. Indoors, they were allowed to put their hair up and wear the latest fashions, but only the women servants, Mrs Waverley, and her like-minded lady friends ever saw them in their best dress.

And what, thought Fanny, is the point of urging

us to spread the word to other women when we are never allowed to talk to anyone other than those dried-up spinsters who frequent Mrs Waverley's tea parties.

It was hard to keep thinking of men as cruel and lustful beasts when the Season began, and at night she could see pretty girls going out from the other houses in the square to balls and parties, all laughing and chattering and excited at the prospect of dancing or flirting with one of those very beasts.

The three Waverley girls had been chosen by Mrs Waverley for their contrasting beauty. Fanny was fair and blue-eyed, Frederica, now eighteen, dark and fiery, and little Felicity, now seventeen, chestnut-haired and willowy.

Fanny did not think much of her own looks, for Mrs Waverley had told her that blondes were sadly unfashionable and there had been no men around to prove to her that a combination of silvery fair hair and sapphire blue eyes was considered bewitching by the highest stickler.

Frederica came into the room, followed by Felicity. Like Fanny, they were dressed to go out in the usual long dark blue cloaks and coal scuttle bonnets.

'You will never guess what I found under Felicity's bed,' crowed Frederica. 'A romance.'

Felicity swung around in a fury. 'You had no right to go poking and prying about my room. How dare you.'

She darted at Frederica to pull her hair, but Frederica scampered off, crying, 'Wait till Mrs

Waverley hears of this!' None of the girls could ever bring themselves to call Mrs Waverley 'Mother'.

With a howl of rage Felicity ran after Frederica. The bell to signal that Mrs Waverley was ready to take them out sounded from the hall below. Fanny sighed. Another day of scraps and quarrels. She wondered how on earth Felicity had managed to get hold of a romance. That was more interesting than the book itself.

She trailed down to the hall. Mrs Waverley unfurled her parasol and said as usual, 'Now, girls, shoulders straight and eyes down. And should any gentleman approach any of you, you are to pretend to be deaf.'

What gentleman was ever going to approach any of them, dressed as they were, thought Felicity gloomily. She had gained a certain distrust of men from Mrs Waverley's teachings. Still, it would be fun to be able to have a chance of spurning one of the monsters.

Out they went into the pale sunlight, Mrs Waverley in front, Fanny behind, then Frederica, then Felicity. But this walk was going to be different.

Fanny did not know it, but this was the walk that was going to change her life.

They were just coming around the square for the fourth time, when a vastly fashionable lady fluttered up to Mrs Waverley and cried, 'It *is* you, is it not? The famous Mrs Waverley?'

Mrs Waverley stopped and looked suspiciously at the exquisite creature that was Lady Artemis. They made an odd contrast. Lady Artemis was wearing a dress of white leno, trimmed with a narrow edging of lace. Around her white shoulders was tied a scarf of pink Italian gauze, fastened on one side with a gold cord, the tassels descending nearly to her feet. She had shoes of the same color, decorated with small gold roses. Keeping her eyes lowered, Fanny gazed at those roses and thought it must be heaven to be allowed to wear anything so frivolous out in the street. Mrs Waverley was a massive woman like the figurehead on a four-master. She had a large face and heavy chin and thick white skin. Her masses of brown hair streaked with gray were confined under a bonnet every bit as unfashionable and depressing as the bonnets the girls wore.

'I am she,' said Mrs Waverley stiffly.

Pansy brown eyes gazed worshipfully at Mrs Waverley as Lady Artemis breathed, 'The famous Rights for Women Mrs Waverley?'

Mrs Waverley visibly unbent. 'I have that modest reputation,' she said.

'Oh, that I could sit at your feet and hear your words of wisdom,' cried Lady Artemis. 'I am a widow, too. Allow me to present myself – Lady Artemis Verity. So we widows know more than anyone the pain of being under the cruel domination of a man.'

'Quite so,' said Mrs Waverley. 'We must teach our sisters that it is possible for women to live free of the shackles of bondage. Men! Pah! We spurn them. We can exist in the sunlight, away from their shadow.'

'If only we could talk longer,' breathed Lady

Artemis. At that moment a handsome guards officer rode past and raised his hat. With a stern effort Lady Artemis prevented herself from smiling at him.

'I am having a little soirée for like-minded ladies on Saturday,' said Mrs Waverley. 'You are more than welcome to attend. Eight o'clock.'

Lady Artemis thought of the Cordeys' ball, which was to be held at the same time. Then she thought of the Earl of Tredair and smiled bewitchingly on Mrs Waverley. 'And if it is not too much to ask, Mrs Waverley, I would like to bring a friend who has like-minded views but is starved for intellectual conversation.'

By now Mrs Waverley was almost purring. 'Bring your friend by all means, Lady Artemis.'

Lady Artemis decided to take her leave quickly before Mrs Waverley asked the identity of this friend. 'Thank you! Thank you!' cried Lady Artemis, sweeping a court curtsy. 'Good-bye. *A bientôt!*'

The procession moved on.

When they entered the house, Mrs Waverley summoned her housekeeper, Mrs Ricketts, a formidable lady who acted as a sort of female butler. 'We have just met a certain Lady Artemis Verity,' said Mrs Waverley, 'who is desirous to attend my soirée on Saturday. Find out about her and make sure she is not a fortune hunter.'

'I'll send Martha,' said Mrs Ricketts. 'She'll soon find out.'

Lady Artemis was sure that Mrs Waverley would send some servant across the square to question her own servants. So she summoned her most handsome footman, Frank, and told him to loiter outside the house and tell anyone who asked that his mistress was a bluestocking, a man-hater, and a terrifying intellectual. After half an hour she had the satisfaction of seeing a dowdy maid leaving Mrs Waverley's, coming around the square, and falling into conversation with Frank.

Frederica had not told Mrs Waverley about Felicity's romance, and so the sisters were in one of their rare, friendly moods when they gathered in the drawing room with their sewing. For a long while the afternoon passed pleasantly enough, until Fanny said, '*I* don't think that Lady Artemis is interested in women's rights or anything other than how to entrap a man.'

'You're jealous,' said Frederica, but without rancor. 'Did you mark her gown? I could have ripped it off her back.'

'We have very pretty gowns of our own,' pointed out Felicity, 'and heaps of jewels.'

'But we're not allowed to wear them when anyone can see them,' pointed out Fanny.

'Oh, yes we are,' said Felicity. 'We get to wear them at Mrs Waverley's soirées. *You* mean that *men* never get to see them.'

Mrs Waverley glided majestically into the room. 'Fanny was just saying that men never get to see our pretty clothes,' said Felicity maliciously.

'I did not!' retorted Fanny hotly.

'You said that no one ever got to see us in our

15

pretty clothes,' said Felicity gleefully, 'and since dear Mrs Waverley's friends always see us in our pretty clothes, who else can you mean but *men*!'

Fanny reddened. 'Come with me, Fanny,' said Mrs Waverley severely, 'and we shall have a little talk.'

When she had left the room with Fanny, Frederica said, 'You little cat. I shall tell her about that romance you are reading, damned if I don't.'

'You said a bad word,' yelled Felicity. 'I shall tell on you.'

They flew at each other and were soon rolling around on the floor, punching and pummeling. In truth, all the girls were dreadfully spoiled by boredom and by the unnaturally cloistered life they led and by the machinations of their protectress, who had brought them up to spy and tell tales on each other.

Downstairs in the library, Fanny sat with head bowed as a lecture on the iniquities of the male sex was poured into her ears.

Fanny tried to remember the horrors of the orphanage, she tried to remember how grateful to Mrs Waverley she must always be, but that day she felt the beginnings of hot rebellion starting somewhere in the pit of her stomach. She, Fanny, wanted to wear pink silk shoes with gold roses and drive in the park in a pink silk-lined chariot drawn by four milk-white horses and have *men* look at her, lots and lots of men.

That feeling of rebellion grew and grew as Saturday approached. On Friday evening she felt restless and on fire. She took her bed candle and crept along the

16

corridor to Felicity's room and searched under the bed, finding nothing more interesting than the chamber pot. Then she slid her hand gently under Felicity's pillow and felt the sharp edges of a book. She drew it out and crept back to her room and started to read her first romance.

In later years she was to smile at her folly and think what a really stupid book it had been. But that night it seemed the most wonderful love story in the world. She read and read until the red dawn crept into the room and the sooty birds began to chirp on the eaves outside.

She managed to catch some much needed sleep that day by pretending to be bent over her sewing while, in fact, being fast asleep. When the dressing bell rang, she felt gritty and tired and almost ill with all the new emotions surging through her body.

Less than ever did there seem to be any point in getting all dressed up for a crowd of women, but Fanny knew that if she did not wear her best, then Mrs Waverley would send her back upstairs to put it on.

She donned a dress of spotted India muslin with puckered sleeves and the front richly ornamented with silver trimming and lace. Over the dress she wore a Persian robe of rich-figured amber sarcenet, made without sleeves and loose from the shoulder. Then she put on a girdle and armlets of gold studded with rubies. White shoes and gloves completed the ensemble. There was a turban encircled with a rouleau of silver muslin to go with the dress, but Fanny put it to one side, dressing her blond hair in one of the Grecian styles and ornamenting it with a gold circlet.

Fanny went slowly down the steps. How wonderful it would be if one of those despised and terrible men were waiting in the hall for her. But when she entered the drawing room, there was only the usual collection. Apart from her sisters, there was Miss Pursy, faded and genteel, Miss Baxter, fat and ferociously jolly, and wispy little Miss Dunbar.

Mrs Waverley was standing in front of the fireplace. 'Now that Fanny has deigned to join us,' she said coldly, 'I shall commence our soirée with a reading from the poem, "The Rights of Women" by Anna Laetitia Barbauld. Ahem.'

'Are we not to wait for Lady Artemis?' asked Fanny.

'It is now two minutes past eight o'clock,' said Mrs Waverley. 'If she is not here now, she is not one of us. Procrastination is the thief of time. I shall begin. Ahem!

Yes, injured Woman! rise, assert thy right!
Woman! too long degraded, scorned, oppressed;
O born to rule in partial Law's despite,
Resume thy native empire o'er the breast!

Go forth arrayed in panoply divine,
That angel pureness which admits no stain;
Go, bid proud Man his boasted rule resign
And kiss the golden sceptre of thy reign.

18

'What is it, Ricketts?'

'Beg parding, mum,' said the flustered house-keeper. 'But that Lady Artemis is come.'

'Then send her in.'

'Please, mum, she's brought a friend with her.'

'What ails you, Ricketts. Send them both in.'

'But, mum . . .'

'Don't stand there, mopping and mowing like an idiot, send them in.'

'Don't say I didn't try to warn you,' said Mrs Ricketts.

A few moments later the double doors to the drawing room were thrown open.

TWO

The Earl of Tredair was highly amused by the atmosphere of shock among the women servants. 'I fear I am about to get my marching orders,' he murmured to Lady Artemis as they stood in the hall.

He was regretting having come. He did not want to establish any intimacy with Lady Artemis. Yet, he had made a bet with her and he was honor bound to stand by it, and the one way he could judge whether Mrs Waverley was the genuine article or not was by meeting her in person.

That Mrs Waverley was very rich could be judged by the expensive tiling on the floor of the hall, by the thick red carpet on the stairs, and by the fine portraits and landscapes decorating the walls. There were bowls of hyacinths scenting the air, and he was surrounded by all the hush of a well-run home.

Ricketts, the housekeeper, descended the stairs.

'My lord, my lady, follow me,' she said, and led the way up to the drawing room on the first floor.

Throwing open the double doors, she announced with relish, 'The most noble Earl of Tredair and Lady Artemis Verity.'

Lord Tredair bowed and looked curiously at the assembled females. A heavy matron was standing in front of the fireplace, a book of poetry in her hands. Three faded spinsters sat looking at him as if Satan himself had descended among them. Then his eyebrows rose as he took in the presence of three young and beautiful girls. Where were the schoolgirls Lady Artemis had described to him earlier that evening when he had called for her?

There was an exquisite blonde with deep-blue eyes and a delicate rose petal complexion, a black-haired beauty with blue eyes and an oval face, and then, obviously the youngest of the three, one with chestnut hair and wide hazel eyes. All were wearing the latest and most expensive of fashions, and all, even the youngest, had an air of good breeding.

Mrs Waverley took a deep breath and summoned up her courage to ban this . . . this *man* from her house when little Miss Dunbar, her faded eyes sparkling and wisps of hair escaping from her pins, said, 'You must make the introductions, Mrs Waverley. What *will* his dear lordship think of us all?'

There was a general fluttering of agreement from the other females, with the exception of the cool blonde.

'I think Lord Tredair has made a mistake,' said

Mrs Waverley awfully. 'We meet here in my little salon to discuss the rights of women . . .'

'A subject very close to my heart, which is why I am come,' said the earl with a bow.

'Our hostess is quite overcome,' said Miss Baxter with a jolly laugh. To Mrs Waverley's fury, she made the introductions. Fanny was bitterly amused. What had happened to all their beliefs and principles? Frederica and Felicity were stifling giggles, Miss Pursy was fluttering about repeating all the introductions, and Miss Dunbar was tripping over chairs in her excitement.

Mrs Waverley moved forward to take over. His lordship would soon find he had come to the wrong house. Lady Artemis had turned out to be a snake in the grass. She noticed that Fanny was not at all impressed and her heart overflowed with love. Dear Fanny. Better than any other girl. Beautiful Fanny.

'If you will be seated here, Lady Artemis,' said Mrs Waverley, all but pushing that lady into a seat by the fireplace, 'and my lord, here, I think, by little Fanny.'

Lady Artemis was still recovering from the shock presented by this barrage of beauty. 'Are the three other girls in the schoolroom?' she asked.

'I have no other girls,' said Mrs Waverley.

'But I met you with three schoolgirls in the square!'

'You met my daughters,' said Mrs Waverley. 'The only ones I have. Now, if you are all ready, I will begin reading again.'

The earl stole a glance at Fanny, who was sitting demurely next to him, her gloved hands resting on her lap. He found it an effort not to stare openly at so much golden beauty. Her hair was so fair, it was almost silver, and curled naturally with that springiness that no amount of curl papers or heated clay rollers could produce. It was free of pomatum, unlike Lady Artemis's hair, which gleamed with oil. Her nose was small and straight, and her startlingly deep blue eyes were fringed with sooty lashes. He wondered if she darkened them and immediately decided she did not. There was nothing artificial about Fanny's beauty. Her gown, as was the fashion, was low cut, revealing the top halves of two excellent white and rounded breasts. Her mouth was soft and pink and well shaped.

Mrs Waverley finished her poetry reading and there was a spattering of applause. 'Now,' said Mrs Waverley, 'our topic for discussion is the education of women.'

'Most important,' said Lady Artemis, flashing a wicked look at Lord Tredair, a look which Fanny intercepted. 'An unaccomplished female is a bore. One should be able to play the pianoforte and to sing.'

'I think,' said the earl, 'that Mrs Waverley means education in Greek and Latin and the sciences.'

'But woman's sole purpose in life is to get married!' cried Lady Artemis.

'And to have children,' pointed out Frederica.

'Exactly,' said Lady Artemis, giving her a warm smile.

'So,' said Frederica, 'it surely follows that an

23

intelligent and well-educated mother will be a better example to her children than an ill-educated and ill-informed one.'

'I disagree,' said Lady Artemis, glancing at the earl for approval. 'Of what use is Greek and Latin when there is a household to run? I would have thought a sound education in housewifery of more importance.'

'Very important,' agreed Felicity, 'but a certain housewifery of the mind is essential or the woman, when her children have grown, may find she has no intellectual reserves for her old age. Come, Lady Artemis, you have seen them in society – the faded lilies of the field who lie on their sofas all day long, vainly trying to amuse themselves with pug dogs and romances.' This was a fair description of Lady Artemis's afternoons, and she looked at Felicity in high irritation as if thinking the girl had been spying on her.

'Aren't you too young to wear your hair up?' snapped Lady Artemis. 'And it is not the thing for young misses to wear jewels.' Felicity had a very fine collar of emeralds about her slim neck.

'It is not at all the thing for young ladies to be educated either,' said Felicity, delighted that their beautiful and worldly guest was behaving so badly. 'But it is time these unwritten and stupid laws were broken.'

Miss Pursy gave a genteel cough. 'I think we are forgetting the gentlemen's point of view,' she said, flashing a flirtatious glance at the earl and earning herself scowls from all around the room. 'They surely are only attracted to ladies who are pretty and fluttery and say babyish things.'

'Not at all,' countered Lady Artemis. 'It is possible to talk well and wittily about plays and operas and Lord Byron's latest poem without having to addle one's brain with a lot of useless science and dead languages.'

' *"Qui finem quaerus amoris, cedet amor rebus; res age, tutus eris,"* ' said the earl. 'Is that what you ladies mean, Miss Fanny?'

There was a little silence. The earl wondered whether this blond goddess was going to ignore him. He wanted to hear her speak. He had maliciously quoted Ovid, feeling perfectly sure that she would not know what he was talking about.

'What did his lordship say?' asked Felicity. 'I did not catch it.'

'My lord was quoting Ovid,' said Fanny. 'Translated, it means, "You who seek an end of love, love yields to business; be busy, and you will be safe." And by that you have betrayed yourself, my lord. Because we support the movement which demands more freedom for women and more education for women, you assume that we must have banished romance and marriage from our minds. You suggest then that we should be busy about our household chores and our sewing to keep softer and feminine thoughts at bay. That is not so. We would be happy were there more gentlemen to share our views, but as there are not, we shun their company. We merely try to instruct other females so that we may bring about a bloodless revolution. It takes a great deal of courage and often leaves us open to ridicule.'

'Dear me,' said the earl acidly – for he had never been put down before, 'you paint a frightening picture of an Almack's full of young misses haranguing us on world affairs.'

Fanny turned and smiled at him, an imp of mischief dancing in her blue eyes. 'It is natural, my lord, that men who are ignorant themselves should view with some degree of jealousy and alarm any proposal for improving the education of women. But such men may depend upon it: however the system of female education may be exalted, that there never will be wanting a due proportion of failure. After parents, guardians, and preceptors have done everything in their power to make everybody wise, there will still be a plentiful supply of women who have taken special care to remain otherwise.' Her blue glance flicked in the direction of Lady Artemis. 'If the great extinction of ignorance and folly is the evil they dread, they should be comforted by the thought that there will always be women who will protect their interests and share their medieval views despite all exertions to the contrary.'

'My dear Miss Fanny,' exclaimed Lady Artemis, 'what a tedious bore you make it all sound. Is there no room for frivolity, dances, masquerades?'

'But of course,' began Fanny, but was frowned into silence by Mrs Waverley. Fanny often argued that their cloistered life was a sham and showed a lack of courage. They had no hope of advocating the independence of women if they sat mewed up in Hanover Square and showed the world not only that they were afraid of men, but afraid of enjoying themselves.

'All frivolity is tedious to the educated mind,' said Mrs Waverley severely.

'But you go too far,' pursued Lady Artemis. 'You have three beautiful daughters. Why do you dress them so drably and allow them only one little walk in the outside world each day? Do you not want to spread your message among the ladies of the ton? Who has ever heard of you?'

'You, for example,' bridled Mrs Waverley, remembering the blandishments of their first meeting.

'Yes, of course,' said Lady Artemis hurriedly, 'but I am not in the ordinary mold. Would you not say so, Lord Tredair?'

'By no means,' he said gallantly. 'Your charm and beauty set you apart from most.'

Frederica and Felicity promptly dismissed him as a useless fop. And yet there was nothing of the fop about the earl with his athletic body, beautiful legs, and clever face. But they had judged him to be the property of Lady Artemis and if he could favor *her*, he was beneath their interest.

'*Now,*' said Mrs Waverley, 'we have a treat in store. Miss Dunbar is to read us her latest poem.'

Lady Artemis rolled her eyes to heaven. 'What a fascinating evening,' murmured the earl to Fanny. 'I have never experienced anything quite like it before.'

'Serves you right,' said Fanny, looking amused.

'But now that you and Lady Artemis have satisfied your curiosity, why do you not take your leave?'

'How can I tear myself away from such beauty as yours?' he said.

'That sounds like a plaster,' said Fanny equably.

'I beg your pardon?'

'When you rise to leave, my lord, I expect to hear a ripping sound as you tear yourself away.'

'Really, Miss Fanny . . .'

'Shhh! Miss Dunbar is about to begin.'

'I thought of this poem,' said Miss Dunbar, looking modestly down her nose, 'when my watch was returned to me from the mender. It is entitled "On a Watch – That Had Been Repaired, Being Hung Up Again in Its Case."'

Welcome, welcome, little stranger,
To thy neat and safe abode;
There thou art, quite free from danger,
There is naught to incommode.

A snort of laughter from Frederica, quickly stifled.

O! how often have I miss'd thee,
Sought in vain the time to know,
And still oftn'er have I wish'd thee
Back, to see thy movements flow.

Days, hours, and minutes, as they pass,
Thou faithfully dost tell,
And art a warning to mankind
To spend e'en moments well.

All the ladies, except Lady Artemis, clapped enthusiastically.

'What a gift education is to women,' mocked the earl, leaning toward Fanny.

'It certainly is,' said Fanny. 'There was a time when poor little Miss Dunbar could barely even write her own name. She has learned much from Mrs Waverley. Her father was a brute and refused to pay a penny on educating his daughters.'

The earl promptly felt every bit as churlish as he was sure Fanny had meant him to feel.

There was more poetry reading. The earl hoped Fanny would perform, but she sat on beside him, sedate and unruffled.

Then Mrs Waverley announced there would be a break for refreshments. Felicity would play for them. The earl sat back, prepared for refreshments such as they served at Almack's, and for the indifferent playing of Felicity who would no doubt hammer out some piece like 'The Woodpecker'.

But Felicity began to play a piece by Scarlatti with such verve and polish that he sat up straight and, almost without thinking, held up his hand for silence. If this is what education does for women, he thought dreamily, then let there be more of it, unaware that his absorption in the music had roused the first feelings of unease in Fanny's bosom. Fanny was jealous, but did not know it. Before the arrival of Lord Tredair, the only man who had been allowed in the house was the music teacher, an elderly German of superb talent. But that stab of unrecognized jealousy made

Fanny painfully aware of the earl for the first time. Here was a man who exuded a male aura of virility, making the high-ceilinged drawing room appear small and cluttered and overfeminine with its pretty gold and white striped curtains and its dainty china figurines. Fanny was glad the musical entertainment was of short duration. Too much attention, she told herself firmly, was bad for Felicity.

To the earl's surprise the refreshments consisted of iced champagne, crab patties, cheese puffs, cold lobster salad, and thin wafers of Westphalian ham served with slices of near transparent bread and butter. He noticed that the three Waverley girls all drank champagne as did the three visiting spinsters.

Emboldened by the wine, Miss Dunbar, Miss Baxter, and Miss Pursy all tried to engage the earl in conversation. But he would answer their sallies politely and then turn back to Fanny.

Poor Fanny's equanimity had gone. His presence was making her feel stifled and overpowered and sick. Her legs trembled and she jammed her knees together.

'Do you think I can persuade your mother to let you go about in society?' asked the earl.

'Mrs Waverley is not my mother. I am adopted, as are the others,' said Fanny. 'We were all taken from the orphanage – a very *low* sort of orphanage,' she added severely, hoping unconsciously to give him a disgust of her so that he would not look at her with that caressing expression in his eyes that made her feel so weak.

'You are fortunate. Where does Mrs Waverley come from? I am not familiar with the family.'

'Mrs Waverley is from Scarborough. Her late husband was extremely rich, and on his death she gained her freedom and was able to do as she wished.'

'I would not like to be married to a lady who regarded my death as a release from bondage.'

'Naturally not,' said Fanny, 'but that is how most women feel about marriage.'

'You must be quoting Mrs Waverley. You do not seem to be allowed to meet other women – I mean, married women.'

'I would . . . well, I confess I would like to go out to a theater or a party, just once,' said Fanny wistfully. 'But perhaps Mrs Waverley is right. Gentlemen in society can be so cruel.'

'For example?'

'For example, there are many children fathered out of wedlock by members of the ton.'

'True. There are a great deal more fathered out of wedlock by everyone else.'

'But not in such a high-handed manner,' said Fanny desperately.

He smiled into her eyes. 'Miss Fanny, I long to hear you describe a high-handed seduction.'

'Oh, you are determined not to take me seriously.'

'I take you more and more seriously by the minute, I assure you. Give me another example of the wanton cruelty of society.'

'Well, there was the case of Mrs Comfrey, a widow who lives in Berners Street. 'Tis said she snubbed

31

young Lord Palmont at a ball. He dressed himself up in butler's livery and went from shop to shop, ordering everything he could think of in her name, and directed it all to her home in Berners Street – even a coffin! The street was blocked for the whole day, and the hysterical lady was beset by tradesmen of every description, porters, medical men, artists, servants wanting places, until the whole of Berners Street was like a fair, it was so crammed with people and wagon loads of goods. Every police officer that could be found was ordered to the area, but it was nightfall before the poor lady could get any peace.'

'A childish joke, I grant you. But hear the other side of the story. Lord Palmont proposed marriage to Mrs Comfrey and was accepted. She did not just snub him, she told him most cruelly, in front of a listening audience of fashionables, that she had changed her mind, he was not good enough for her. He protested. She went on to maliciously describe his physical defects, ending up by announcing with a coarse laugh that he wore false calves.'

'Oh, dear,' said Fanny. 'Then, perhaps it is as well I do not go about in society, for the women appear to be as bad as the men. You yourself and Lady Artemis came this evening out of vulgar curiosity. Neither of you gives a fig for the plight of the modern woman.'

'Nor does Mrs Waverley. I am persuaded she is secretly a timid woman who has bought love and loyalty from the orphanage and does not dare go about lest she lose her court.'

'I am persuaded you do not know the first thing about love and loyalty,' said Fanny fiercely.

His eyes caressed her furious face. 'On the contrary, I do know a great deal about love.'

'I was not talking about either lust or sexual experience,' flashed Fanny.

Unfortunately, her voice had risen at the moment when everyone else in the room had stopped talking.

There was a shocked silence.

The earl rose to his feet and bowed in front of Mrs Waverley. 'My congratulations on the education of your girls,' he said. 'Such wit and grace and style! I am quite overwhelmed.'

'Fanny . . .' said Mrs Waverley desperately. She had not been able to believe her ears. 'You must apologize.'

'No need for apology,' said the earl with a mocking smile. 'Miss Fanny is as you have made her. How wise of you to keep her locked up. Lady Artemis! We shall take our leave.'

'Gladly!' said Lady Artemis, tossing her head.

Fanny sat with her head bowed as the guests left.

Out in the square, Lady Artemis looked up at the earl, who was escorting her across the square to her home. 'Can I persuade you to return and share my tea tray?'

'No, my lady. I am going to my club to immerse myself in the company of men. But I shall send you a hundred guineas.'

'Generous of you. But I feel it is *I* who should pay you,' said Lady Artemis. 'I am persuaded they are all frauds and none more than the beautiful and farouche Miss Fanny.'

'Perhaps. But I cannot remember when I was last so well entertained,' said the earl. He touched his hat with his gloves and strode off across the square.

Lady Artemis went slowly indoors. That was that. He would smile at her and nod to her across some ballroom, but unless she plotted and planned, she had no hope of being in his company again.

The evening had been strangely exhilarating. Funny, ridiculous, infuriating, but not boring. The key to Lord Tredair's flinty heart lay with the Waverleys. He seemed to mock them, he had been furious with Fanny, but Fanny had kept her by him for the whole evening. So education was the clue. What had Fanny been talking about before she had made that dreadful social gaffe? The only way to find out was to cultivate the Waverleys.

Lady Artemis thought of her own conversation. Usually she gossiped, passing around the latest *on-dit* when she found herself in the company of women, which was seldom. With the men she talked light nonsense and flirted.

Her butler relieved her of her cloak and stood waiting for orders.

'Have all the morning papers delivered to me in my bedchamber at nine in the morning with my chocolate,' said Lady Artemis. The butler blinked. Nine o'clock was dawn in fashionable London. 'And hire me tutors. I have to learn Greek and Latin. And I need a music teacher. A good music teacher. I want

34

to play complicated and difficult pieces. And go to the shoemaker in the morning and bring him around here to measure my feet. I want walking shoes.'

'Yes, my lady,' said the butler gloomily, for, as he confided to the other servants, my lady was probably as drunk as a lord and would throw things at his head when she was awakened at nine in the morning.

The following morning, after the chambermaid had lit the fire in my lady's room and opened the shutters and drawn back the curtains, the butler entered carrying the requested cup of hot chocolate and nine morning papers.

Lady Artemis was lying snoring, her mouth open. One white breast had popped out of her nightgown, and the nipple stared up at the butler like one accusing eye.

If he woke her and she found that naked breast, then he would be dismissed for looking at her. And yet it was forbidden for a manservant to touch his mistress's bare flesh. The chambermaid was too lowly a creature to do it. The lady's maid was in bed with the grippe. Problems, problems, thought the butler with a sigh. He took out a clean white handkerchief, covered his hand with it, and, leaning over the bed, tucked the bare breast out of sight. Then he coughed loudly.

Lady Artemis came awake and glared at him and then glared at the clock. Then memory came flooding back. She struggled up against the pillows, took the proferred newspapers, and began to read.

'Must be love,' thought the butler. 'She's fallen for a pedant. It won't last a day.'

At two o'clock Mrs Waverley appeared, but with only two girls following her. She found to her annoyance that Lady Artemis appeared to have sprung from nowhere and had joined them.

'And where is Miss Fanny this morning?' asked Lady Artemis.

'She is in disgrace,' said Mrs Waverley. 'It all goes to prove my point that the company of gentlemen is destructive.'

'To one who has not been trained in the arts of social conversation,' said Lady Artemis impatiently. 'My dear Mrs Waverley, if I may be so bold, you scuttle around this square like a mother hen. No wonder your daughters have become odd and unruly.'

Mrs Waverley stopped so suddenly that Frederica and Felicity bumped into her.

Lady Artemis waited curiously. She wondered whether Mrs Waverley had gone into a trance.

Mrs Waverley was thinking deeply. Fanny's bold and brazen remark to Lord Tredair had shocked her. She had been proud of her girls, considering them paragons of all the virtues. She could not bear failure and detected a certain amused contempt in Lady Artemis's eyes.

'Courage,' murmured Lady Artemis, when Mrs Waverley did not speak. 'The Park is beautiful this afternoon. Why not promenade with me a little farther?'

Mrs Waverley still stood as if turned to stone. She

wanted to refuse. She wanted to berate Lady Artemis for having brought a man into her salon. But for the first time in years, she felt ridiculous and eccentric.

'Besides,' cooed Lady Artemis, 'I did not come last night to mock you, Mrs Waverley. But to learn. You appear to think you have a mission to educate women. Would you spurn me – I, who have so much to learn?'

Mrs Waverley took a deep breath. 'Very well, Lady Artemis. What is it you would like to learn first?'

All at once Lady Artemis thought of those house-keeping books that she could never check because she could not add figures. 'Mathematics,' she said with a laugh. 'But you will need to begin at the beginning.'

Fanny looked down from her bedroom window. She could see Lady Artemis talking to Mrs Waverley with Frederica and Felicity standing behind them. Soon, thought Fanny, they would move; the snubbed Lady Artemis would go back to her home and the other three back to walking around and around the square. Then to her surprise, they all moved off together and disappeared out of the square.

She was furious. The first steps into the outside world had been taken without her. She would not admit to herself that most of her fury was caused by the unrealized thought that in that outside world somewhere was the Earl of Tredair. Fanny had been told to stay in her room all day as a punishment. She longed to run after them, to disobey. But at the back of her mind, there was always the fear that Mrs

Waverley might send her back to the orphanage. Well, she could hardly send a great nineteen-year-old back there, but she could just send her away.

Fanny wanted to rebel, but she was not ready yet.

The Earl of Tredair was sitting in his club in the coffee room, reading the newspapers. He liked his club. He liked it best during the day when it had a cathedral-like hush and the gentle, dismal peace of one great communal hangover dwelt in the high-ceilinged rooms.

His peace was disturbed by the arrival of his friend, the Honorable John Fordyce who plumped himself down in a chair opposite and exclaimed, 'I have seen a most odd sight.'

'What?' asked the earl irritably. 'Some freak? The man with the two-headed cow?'

'Better than that. I crossed the Park a short time ago, and there, under a tree on a park bench, I saw the beautiful Lady Artemis. She was seated beside a fat, dowdy matron and two drab schoolgirls, and you will never guess what she was doing.'

'No, I can't guess. Put me out of my misery.'

'She was reciting her multiplication tables – you know, like in a schoolroom, with the fat woman and the girls chanting along with her. Two times two is four and all that.'

'Two schoolgirls,' said the earl slowly. 'Not three?'

'No, two. And Lady Artemis . . .'

'Was one of the girls divinely fair?'

'No, I tell you, just two drab little girls and I could

38

not tell the color of their hair, for they wore the ugliest bonnets I have ever seen.'

'So fair Fanny's probably in disgrace,' mused the earl aloud. 'Good! Serves her right.'

'What are you talking about? Do you know such people?'

'I know a surprising number of oddities,' said the earl, and changed the subject.

THREE

The Earl of Tredair had hit on the correct reason for
Mrs Waverley's seclusion. She was at heart a timid
woman who not only feared the world of men, but
the rest of the world at large. She had used her great
wealth to buy herself companionship in the shape
of the three girls and to buy the house in Hanover
Square to keep all the things she feared at bay.

She was herself a highly educated woman with a
gift for teaching. Despite the fact that Lady Artemis
was using Mrs Waverley in order to see the Earl of
Tredair again, that frivolous creature of society had
to admit to a certain feeling of exhilaration as the
days passed and the lessons continued and all those
mysterious figures began to make sense.

Gratitude to Mrs Waverley, plus a desire to further
her own ends, prompted Lady Artemis to set about
encouraging her teacher to go out into the world a

little more. Finally, she was rewarded. Mrs Waverley agreed to attend a performance of *Richard III*. All young ladies should see Shakespeare performed on the stage, said Lady Artemis, and Mrs Waverley caved in and told her startled daughters of the treat in store.

Although she was delighted at the idea of going out to the theater, Fanny could not like the person who had arranged it. She distrusted Lady Artemis and jealousy had sharpened her perceptions so that she felt Lady Artemis was using them all to recapture Lord Tredair's attention.

The girls did not have a lady's maid, Mrs Waverley feeling that lady's maids were flighty creatures too interested in men. Fanny dressed herself with great care. The girls were not only to be allowed to go to the theater, but to appear at their best.

She chose a pale pink gossamer silk gown, ornamented with a narrow gold edging and tied at the front with ribbons of the same color. On her head she wore a headdress composed of white lace and pink satin, ornamented with double rows of pearls. Around her neck she wore a necklace of fine pearls set in gold.

She wondered feverishly whether the earl would be there and then tried to dismiss him from her mind. She had been rude to him and he probably thought of her, if he thought of her at all, with disgust. He would not be there.

But the earl, too, was preparing to go to the theater. He had received a note from Lady Artemis that had

41

said, 'Do you attend Kean in *Richard*? If so, I have a marvel to show you that will not be on the stage.'

'By which,' the earl said cynically to Mr Fordyce, 'she means she has somehow managed to persuade that recluse you saw in the Park and her three girls to go.'

'Tell me about the recluse,' asked Mr Fordyce curiously. He had come to accompany his friend to the playhouse. 'And I only saw two girls.'

'Her name is Mrs Waverley, and she is a staunch supporter of the rights of women. She lives in seclusion in Hanover Square with three adopted daughters. It would appear that Lady Artemis has befriended her. I am only guessing, of course. But I shall be very surprised if Mrs Waverley is not the promised treat.'

'By why should Lady Artemis think you would be interested in a recluse with an interest in bluestocking matters?'

'Lady Artemis took me to a soirée at the Waverley house. I was amused and infuriated. She no doubt thinks I want to be amused and infuriated again. Perhaps she is right.'

'Are you . . . em . . . *interested* in Lady Artemis?' asked Mr Fordyce. 'She is all that is beautiful and kind.'

'No, despite the fact that she is beautiful. I doubt whether she is kind.'

'Then there is hope for me if you are not taken with her,' sighed Mr Fordyce.

'Every hope,' said the earl cheerfully.

'Not with my undistinguished appearance,' mourned Mr Fordyce. 'Oh, that I could look like you for just one evening!' He glanced enviously at his tall friend's impeccable tailoring and broad-shouldered, slim-hipped muscular figure.

'Fustian, you look very well,' said the earl. 'And you are too good a man for such as Lady Artemis. She is shallow.'

'I am persuaded you are too hard.'

'Let us not quarrel. We shall be late if we do not leave now.'

The earl drew on his gloves and tucked his bicorne under his arm and led the way downstairs.

Fanny, Frederica, and Felicity all felt like freaks as they sat in Lady Artemis's box at the playhouse. Opera glasses, quizzing glasses, and even small telescopes were trained on their box.

Frederica and Felicity blushed miserably, glancing down at their gowns as if expecting to find something wrong. Lady Artemis lazily fanned herself and smiled all around. The Waverley girls were a sensation.

It was only when the earl's tall figure appeared in a box opposite that Lady Artemis felt a good deal of her complacency leaving her. She felt a trifle soiled and, yes, *old* alongside this dazzling bevy of fresh beauties who sat grouped together like some nosegay with flowerlike complexions and gleaming hair.

She comforted herself with the thought that such a sophisticated man of the world as the earl would not be intrigued by a parcel of young virgins. She had expected him to be amused and interested, not attracted. But Fanny had kept him at her side that evening, and Fanny's looks were certainly enough to break hearts. Lady Artemis knew that blondes were not fashionable, but Fanny's combination of silvery hair and deep blue eyes and black lashes was causing men in the pit to stand up on their benches for a better look.

To Fanny's relief when the curtain rose, a hush fell on the house. Edmund Kean as Richard III limped slowly down the stage. He looked up at the boxes with an expression of sly cunning, and then he began. 'Now is the winter of our discontent . . .'

Fanny, like the rest of the house, was held captive by the great actor. Usually society came to the playhouse to see each other and the only attention they gave the performance was to catcall or throw oranges at the stage. But Kean held them all in the palm of his hand.

At the first interval the earl and Mr Fordyce made their way to Lady Artemis's box. But they had to wait outside until almost the end of the interval, there was such a press of gentlemen anxious to pay their respects to Lady Artemis and to get an introduction to the Waverley girls.

At last Mr Fordyce and the earl edged in. Lady Artemis welcomed the earl warmly so that it was left to Mr Fordyce to talk to the girls. 'What do you think of the performance?' he asked.

Three pairs of glowing eyes looked at him, and

three voices competed to tell him how wonderful Kean was. All the girls appeared to know the play by heart. He was rather intimidated by their direct looks and intelligent speech. Not one blushed or fluttered or raised her fan.

While Fanny talked, she was covertly studying the earl and Lady Artemis. She noticed how Lady Artemis, standing in the box in front of the earl, contrived to make love to him with her body while never touching him. She swayed and undulated as she talked, exclaiming over an imagined rip in her hem so that she could bend over and allow the earl to look down the front of her gown. The enigma that was Mrs Waverley sat quietly, looking on.

The next act was about to begin. The earl and Mr Fordyce excused themselves, promising to call at the second interval.

Fanny was glad to lose herself again in the play. The earl made her feel upset, hot, and uncomfortable. If this is what men did to your body, then you were better without them.

The earl and Mr Fordyce made their way back to Lady Artemis's box just before the end of the second act. The earl tipped an usher to keep all other callers at bay and entered the box just as the curtain fell. Fanny had not once looked in his direction. He decided to get at her through Mrs Waverley. Mr Fordyce was only too eager to speak to Lady Artemis. The earl sat down by Mrs Waverley, who shied like a horse at the sight of him.

'I am glad to see you furthering the education of

your girls in the proper way,' he said. Mrs Waverley majestically inclined her head. 'And surely you must see no harm will come to them.'

'I consider Shakespeare to be part of any young woman's education,' said Mrs Waverley. 'Balls and parties on the other hand have no educational value.'

'I do so agree,' said the earl earnestly. 'You must forgive me if I seemed a trifle sharp the other evening, Mrs Waverley, but Miss Fanny did provoke me.'

He cast a sidelong look at Fanny whose blue eyes blazed at him.

'I accept that Fanny was unusually provoking,' said Mrs Waverley. 'She has been punished.'

'And can we now hope to see you at other events?'

'I do not think so,' said Mrs Waverley. 'Everything else at the Season is a sad waste of time and will only encourage vanity in the bosom of my girls.'

'Not everything,' said the earl. 'There is a balloon ascension in two days time. Now, if you have any interest in the sciences, you must admit a balloon ascension is highly educational.'

'Where is this ascension to take place?' asked Mrs Waverley.

'At Islington. Our famous balloonist, Mr Greene, is to take to the skies. Have you ever attended a balloon ascension?'

'No. I . . .'

'But you must. I insist. Mr Fordyce and myself can escort you there.'

'But, I . . .'

'Splendid. Mr Fordyce, we are in luck. Mrs

46

Waverley and her beautiful charges are to join us in a visit to the balloon ascension.'

'We shall enjoy that,' said Lady Artemis quickly, although she had not been included in the invitation. 'Do wear something warm, ladies. I do not know why it is, but balloon ascensions always seem to take place on the coldest of days.'

The girls' eyes were shining with excitement. The three of them had feared that this was to be their one and only outing. Fanny even began to feel a certain gratitude toward Lady Artemis, who had been instrumental in effecting this change.

'Thank you, but we shall not go,' said Mrs Waverley heavily.

'And why not?' demanded Fanny angrily. If this was the outside world of society, then she loved it. She thought of the long days and months and years spent in seclusion and her beautiful eyes filled with tears. 'You are always telling us about the wonders of science, about ballooning, about how balloons could be used as a military weapon. And yet you lack the courage to allow us to see such miracles for ourselves.'

Frederica's hand stole out to grip Felicity's.

'Balloon ascensions attract a great number of the unruly mob,' pointed out Mrs Waverley, wishing the interval would come to an end.

'But you will be in my carriage and Mr Fordyce's,' pointed out the earl. He took Mrs Waverley's gloved hand in his own and smiled into her eyes. 'Please say you will come.'

'Very well,' said Mrs Waverley weakly. 'Just this once.'

'Bravo! Then we shall call for you at eleven in the morning.'

The earl rose and bowed to everyone and left the box with Mr Fordyce. The third act began, but the earl's thoughts were elsewhere. He was thinking of Fanny and how when her eyes had filled with tears, he had longed to take her in his arms. This yearning, protective feeling was new to him. He was sure that if he got to know Fanny very well, then he would find her boring. By the end of the play he had convinced himself this was the case and regretted his impulse to escort the Waverley ladies.

That night, Fanny tossed and turned, unable to sleep. Excitement gripped her like a fever. She felt she could hardly wait until the balloon ascension to see the proper outside world again. She would not admit to herself she could hardly wait to see Lord Tredair again. 'If only I had something amusing to read, like Felicity's romance,' she thought. Then she began to wonder where on earth Felicity had got that romance.

She got out of bed and went to Felicity's room and pushed open the door. Felicity was lying in bed reading. She had had her bedside oil lamp specially deepened by the tinman so that it would burn all night.

Fanny sat on the end of Felicity's bed. 'How did you come by that romance?' she asked.

Felicity put down her book and looked at Fanny impatiently. 'I went and bought it.'

'But how? We are not allowed out.'

'Well, don't tell anyone. You know after our daily promenade that Mrs Waverley goes for a nap. I simply went out and along to Hatchard's in Piccadilly and bought one.'

'But the women servants are told to stop us from leaving!'

'Stoopid. I go down to the library and let myself out through the window and drop down into the garden. Then I climb over the wall at the side and through the garden of the house adjoining – no one lives there at the moment – and that house has a path around the side to the area steps.'

'But we are not allowed any pin money.'

'We are allowed a great deal of fine jewelry,' said Felicity. 'I simply take a little piece from my box, or prize out a jewel and take it to the pawnbroker in Oxford Street.'

'That's *stealing*,' said Fanny, appalled.

'Not really. She don't miss it and it stops me from going mad.'

'Frederica is surely not a party to this?'

'Oh, yes. She escapes one day and I escape the other.'

'Good gracious,' said Fanny weakly. 'Why didn't you tell me before?'

'You're always so hoity-toity. We thought you'd tell.'

'*I* tell? It is you and Frederica who are always telling on each other.'

'We keep important things secret.'

Fanny looked at Felicity in distress. 'But all our principles, all our ideas.'

'They're Mrs Waverley's principles and ideas,' said Felicity. 'She's a great teacher, I'll grant you that. I like being able to read the classics in the original Greek and Latin, but I also like to read something light and frivolous from time to time to take my mind off the boredom of my existence. Mind you, I don't believe any of this romantic stuff and nonsense. Mrs Waverley is right. It is a man's world and women are little better than slaves. I just don't like the way she keeps us imprisoned. I mean, you support her ideas, too, don't you Fanny?'

'Of course!'

'Not getting a leetle spoony about the handsome earl?'

'Don't be cheeky or I'll punch your head,' said Fanny, her color rising.

'Just try,' grinned Felicity. 'Oh, don't look daggers at me. I'll have a word with Freddy and tell her you can have tomorrow.'

'I don't know whether I will be able to find the courage,' said Fanny weakly. 'Does one just go into the pawnbroker and hand over a jewel?'

'His name is Friendly, a Quaker; a good name for a pawnbroker and a Quaker, don't you think? He believes me to be a servant girl, pawning jewels for my mistress. Her fictitious name is Lady Tremblant. I suggest you use it. After all, those usual ghastly duds we are dressed in for our walks are like servants' clothes.'

* * *

The next day Felicity went straight to her jewel box after their walk around the square. To her relief, Lady Artemis had not joined them. Rubies, diamonds, emeralds, and sapphires glinted up at her. How much would a book cost? She selected a small diamond pin and tucked it inside the neck of her gown and then went down to the drawing room. She felt very tired and half inclined to forget about going ahead with the escapade. Their lessons were given to them by Mrs Waverley at ten o'clock each morning. Felicity looked grumpy having had less sleep than Fanny, but Frederica was excited that the eldest of them, the golden Fanny, was about to behave just as badly.

They took her down to the library on the ground floor and helped her through the window and watched her jump down to the weedy garden below that was on a level with the basement. The servants were taking tea in their hall at the front of the basement and so there was no danger of being discovered. Fanny turned and waved. The girls pointed to an upturned water barrel against the wall, and she climbed up on it and pulled herself to the top of the wall. There was a plank leaning on the other side, and she slid down it and made her way quickly around the side of the empty neighboring house and up the area steps.

At first it seemed terrifying to be out on her own. Oxford Street was crammed with passersby and carriages of every description. Then it dawned on her that everyone was too busy to look at a drably dressed female in a voluminous cloak and depressing hat.

The pawnbroker's three golden balls glinted in the pale sunlight. She pushed open the door and went into the musty interior, which smelled of fried bacon and old clothes.

Barely daring to look at the man behind the counter, she handed over the diamond pin and murmured that her mistress, Lady Tremblant, was in need of more money. 'Five pounds,' said the pawnbroker, beginning to write out a ticket. Fanny looked at him for the first time. He was bent and shabby with a cruel acquisitive look like a bird of prey.

'Nonsense, you scoundrel,' said Fanny haughtily. 'Give it back to me immediately. Thirty pounds and nothing less!'

Fanny did not know that both Frederica and Felicity had affected common accents when they pawned their jewels. The pawnbroker looked at that haughty stare and flashing eyes and came to the conclusion that this must be Lady Tremblant in person. He held the pin up to the light and the diamond flashed fire. It was a fine stone, and he had no wish to offend an aristocratic patron. The stone was worth much, much more than thirty and this Lady Tremblant never redeemed her jewels.

'Did I say five, my lady? I am sorry. I meant thirty-five.'

'Good,' said Fanny icily. 'Now give me my ticket.' She had every intention of trying to redeem the jewel, although where she was going to get the money, she was not quite sure.

She left the shop and took a deep breath. Thirty-five

pounds! A fortune. She was not sure how to get to Hatchard's, or for that matter, Piccadilly, and had to stop and ask the way.

In the bookshop she bought two three volume romances, which she put into her huge reticule. Now for home.

But the sun was shining and the crowds looked so jolly and happy. Fanny had always wanted to go to the Park at the fashionable hour and see all the fine folk. She glanced down at the watch pinned to her bosom. Four-thirty. She had been away from home for more than two hours!

Perhaps if she made a circular detour home, along Piccadilly, up Park Lane, and along through Grosvenor Square and Brook Street, she could maybe catch a glimpse of society at play.

Almost despite herself, her steps took her into the Park and soon she was standing at the edge of the Ring, watching the light-glittering carriages darting past like dragonflies. She was about to turn away when she saw Lord Tredair. She half raised her hand in salute and then let it drop to her side. For he did not see her. He was riding a coal black stallion, and he had reined in beside a carriage containing two beautiful ladies. They were smiling up at him and he looked delighted to see them.

It was then that Fanny realized her own circumstances for the first time. She was a foundling. She had been taken to the foundling hospital from the steps of St Bride's in Fleet Street and then from there to the orphanage. Her parents had probably never married. Her parents were most likely poor and common. If a man such as the earl were interested in her, it would be to purchase her as his mistress.

Sadly, she turned away. She felt miserable. She felt like the thief she was.

Her spirits were hardly rallied on her return when Felicity and Frederica berated her for being so late back and nearly spoiling *their* future plans of escape.

Then, that very evening, Mrs Waverley decided to lecture the girls on the subject of love.

Fanny found that lecture very lowering, although it all sounded like good sense. Women, said Mrs Waverley, usually fell genuinely in love once and then became addicted to the idea of being in love. Romantic love did not last and had no secure foundation. Passion was fleeting. It was a well-known fact that any man tired of the charms of one woman after a time, eighteen months being the longest period. True love was a combination of loyalty and caring. Women should not find it necessary to look to men for such love, when that pure kind of love was something another woman could supply.

'But what about children?' cried Fanny. 'God made us as we are to bear children!'

'God also gave us brains,' said Mrs Waverley. 'Look about you. London is overpopulated with unwanted brats. Why add to the misery?'

Fanny felt very low in spirits when they set out the next day for the balloon ascension, and her spirits were further lowered by the fact that she and Mrs Waverley were to travel in Mr Fordyce's carriage while Felicity and Frederica and Lady Artemis went in the earl's carriage.

'If only men were really like the heroes in books,' thought Fanny before she climbed into Mr Fordyce's carriage, and she cast a yearning look at the earl, who did not notice.

But Felicity did, and she pinched the back of Frederica's hand and whispered, 'Got something to tell you.'

When they reached the fields at Islington where the great balloon was moored, Fanny felt much happier. The earl had appeared at her side and she turned impulsively to him and said, 'Oh, how I should like to fly above the houses. To be free.'

Again, he experienced that odd, protective, yearning feeling. Mr Fordyce was happily lecturing Mrs Waverley and Lady Artemis on the art of ballooning, and Frederica and Felicity were whispering with their heads together. Lady Artemis had decided to try to make the earl jealous by flirting with Mr Fordyce.

'There is our balloonist, Mr Greene,' cried the earl as a carriage drove up. 'Come, Miss Fanny. I have an idea.'

Fanny was introduced to the famous balloonist. 'Mr Greene, with your permission, before you make your ascent,' said the earl, 'may I take Miss Waverley here into the basket so that she may get some idea of what it might be like to fly?'

55

'By all means,' said Mr Greene. 'There's some fellows over there with a ladder.'

Felicity and Frederica watched round-eyed as they saw the earl helping Fanny into the balloon basket. Above them, the great pink and gold balloon soared up to the heavens. 'I tell you, she's spoony about him,' hissed Felicity. 'She's going to run off and get married and I can't bear it. Why should she escape and betray us and our ideas?'

Frederica grinned maliciously. 'Let's give them a fright.'

'What do you mean?'

'I have my sharp knife. We could creep around and fray the ropes so that, perhaps, they might snap and tilt the basket and give Fanny a scare.'

'That won't do any good. They're loaded down with sandbags.'

But as the girls watched, Mr Greene himself climbed into the basket and could be seen explaining the working of the balloon to Fanny. The earl said something and Mr Greene smiled. He and the earl started to throw out sandbags and the crowd cheered as the basket lifted, straining at the ropes.

'Are they taking Fanny up?' asked Felicity.

'No,' said Frederica. 'She'd freeze to death. Mr Green's giving them an idea of what it feels like. See, they're bringing back the ladder. Fanny'll be getting down.'

'Let's give her that fright,' said Frederica. 'You start shouting that someone has stolen Mr Greene's horse and leave the rest to me.'

Frederica darted off. Felicity had no intention of calling Mrs Waverley's attention to herself, so she tugged at the sleeve of a man in front of her and said, 'I just saw a ruffian steal Mr Greene's carriage horse.'

The man immediately shouted out that the horse had been stolen without even looking round to see if the voice at his ear had told the truth. Soon the whole crowd was shouting thief and calling to Mr Greene. The balloonist darted down the ladder. In the commotion Frederica scurried from guy rope to guy rope, sawing busily. In the shouting and running and yelling no one noticed her.

But the day had become wild and blustery and one great buffet of wind struck the balloon. Instead of just one of the guys giving and tipping the basket over, all the ropes snapped at once. The crowd cheered thinking it was some sort of stunt. Mr Greene howled. Mrs Waverley turned white and clutched at Mr Fordyce for support.

The balloon soared straight up and for a moment appeared to hang motionless just a little above the crowd. Fanny looked white and scared, the earl, furious. Then another buffet of wind and the balloon began to sail away rapidly to the east.

A silence fell upon the crowd as it dawned on all of them that the lady and gentleman had been borne off by mistake. They watched anxiously as the balloon grew smaller and smaller until it disappeared behind a bank of clouds.

Several of the men in the crowd removed their

hats and stood with their heads bowed. Few expected amateurs to survive the flight.

Clutching each other, Felicity and Frederica began to cry.

FOUR

Fanny's hands clutched the edge of the balloon basket so tightly that one of her gloves split. The clouds parted, and down below were little fields and little dots of people. The earl was cursing and fiddling with the gas burner. They had changed direction and appeared to be rushing off madly to the west.

'I trust you can get us down,' said Fanny over her shoulder.

'I am trying, Miss Fanny,' he said crossly. 'I know little of ballooning. This is one of the older ones, not hydrogen gas, but hot air. I do not think those ropes parted of their own accord. Someone must have cut them. Are you very cold?'

'Yes,' said Fanny, surprised. She had hitherto been too startled and shocked to realize just how cold she was. She wondered for the first time why Mrs Waverley in all her strictures against the follies of the human race had not thought to attack current fashions. To be dressed in transparent white muslin on a chilly spring day surely suggested a devotion to fashion bordering on the frenetic. Fanny's gown was deeply décolleté, the transparency of the muslin revealing a minimum of pink underclothing, and a slit at the side showing pink stockinged legs. Over it she wore a lace pelisse, and on her head a Mary Queen of Scots cap of white velvet and gold thread.

He took off his coat and wrapped it about her and then returned to fiddling with the burner. A gust of wind seized Fanny's cap and sent it flying and tore the pins from her hair so that it blew about her head and shoulders. She slipped her arms into the sleeves of the coat he had put about her shoulders and peered over the edge of the basket again.

'I am fortunate to be able to have this view of the world,' Fanny told herself. 'I am sure I am not going to die. It is silly to waste an opportunity like this through sheer maidenly weakness and fear. We must be getting lower. People look more like toys than dots. And, I declare, the wind has dropped.'

The basket swung around, and there, revealed on the other side, was a distant line of gray heralding the broad expanse of the sea.

'Miss Fanny!' Fanny edged around and looked at the earl. His green eyes looked bleak. 'I am afraid we may be in for a ducking. I do not suppose you can swim.'

'Yes, I can,' shivered Fanny. 'Do not worry, my

lord, I am not afraid. I cannot possibly feel colder in the water than I do at present.'

He caught her in his arms and held her close as the balloon swayed and turned, getting lower the whole time.

'Turn up the burner!' cried Fanny suddenly. 'That way we shall not continue to sink.'

'My dear child, we shall end up in the middle of the North Sea if I do not get us down soon. The Thames estuary is still directly below us.'

Fanny struggled free and before he could guess what she meant to do, she had wrenched at the gas burner. The flame went out with a noisy pop.

'You half-witted idiot,' howled the earl.

'Stop shouting at me and light it,' snapped Fanny.

'I have neither brimstone match nor tinder-box, but I suppose such an enlightened, modern lady as yourself carries such items.'

He cast a cynical eye at the piece of dainty nonsense that passed for a reticule, dangling from Fanny's wrist.

Fanny bit her lip. Normally she did carry an amount of useful stuff about with her, but vanity had prompted the thin gown and the scrap of a reticule. She realized that trying to compete with Lady Artemis had its drawbacks.

'Well,' he said in a milder tone, 'down we go. Hang onto me . . .'

'No!'

'Don't be silly. If we are plunged into the water

61

upside down or something, you will need all the help I can offer.'

He drew her to him again and held her tightly while the balloon, which had ceased its rushing, plunging motion, drifted down and down.

'I believe we shall make land after all,' he said at last, looking over the top of her head. Fanny pulled free and looked over the edge of the balloon. There was a village below, and she could see faces turned upward and hands pointing. Light glinted from musical instruments as the village band ran this way and that, staring upward, and colliding with each other. A tiny figure in an open carriage, just recognizable as a mayor from one of the neighboring towns, could be seen hurtling along the road to the village.

At first, to Fanny, they seemed to be drifting gently sideways toward the village, and then all at once the balloon gave a lurch and straight down it went. She threw her arms around the earl and clutched him tight.

'Sit down,' he commanded, dragging her down to the bottom of the basket.

They lay in the bottom as close as lovers. There was a sickening bump and then the deflated balloon collapsed on top of the basket.

There were cries and cheers from outside. Dazed and bruised and shaken, Fanny looked up at the earl who was lying on top of her. He grinned suddenly and kissed the tip of her nose and then rolled off her and helped her to her feet, taking his coat from her and putting it on, just as the covering that was the balloon was ripped away and the round red face of the mayor in full ceremonial robes appeared at the top of a ladder.

'I am sorry to have caused so much disturbance,' said the earl, bowing low. 'I am Tredair, Lord Tredair, and this is Miss Fanny Waverley.'

The mayor's red face became even redder with delight. A real live lord!

'Pray descend,' said the mayor, 'and accept the hospitality of this humble village.'

The earl made his way down the ladder and then turned to help Fanny.

A great cheer went up from the villagers, the sun shone, the village band began to play 'Rule Britannia', as Fanny with her golden hair streaming about her shoulders descended from the balloon.

'Speech! Speech!' screamed the villagers.

'Cannot we just go?' whispered Fanny fiercely to the earl.

'No. This is the biggest thing that has ever happened to them and we must not disappoint them,' said the earl and climbed back up the ladder. He noticed ruefully that the road leading to the village was jammed with carriages and hawkers, conjurors and jugglers. Everyone must have been following the progress of the balloon for some time and any excuse for a fair had drawn them all as if pulled by one enormous magnet.

The earl raised his hands for silence. 'Thank you, my lord mayor, and good people of . . .'

'Deep-Under-Lime,' hissed the mayor.

'Deep-Under-Lime,' said the earl.

'And the township of Deep of which I am the mayor,' prompted the mayor, sotto voce.

The earl duly repeated all that and went on, 'Miss Waverley and I are most grateful to you all. We had said our last prayers and had just given ourselves up for dead, when a ray of light struck down from the heavens, right on this village.'

There was an awed gasp.

'The hand of God guided us here,' said the earl. 'In fact, the village of Deep-Under-Lime was chosen by Divine Providence to be our place of rescue. I shall now tell you how we came to be in this predicament . . .'

Fanny listened in horror. How could he tell such lies? Well, not exactly lies, but such a wildly exaggerated tale. A cloud crossed the sun and she shivered. But she could only be glad that the earl was holding his audience. He made a handsome and commanding figure, and he stood with one booted foot upon one rung of the ladder, the wind ruffling his black hair. For just before he had begun to speak, Fanny had noticed the shocked looks cast at her gown. What she was wearing was respectable for a fine lady in London, but here her scanty attire looked more suitable wear for a prostitute.

'At the height of our peril,' the earl was saying, 'a great gust of wind tore Miss Waverley's outer gown from her body. Picture her distress. Her outraged modesty. Perhaps one of you good people could lend her a warm cloak? Thank you.'

Fanny smiled gratefully at the better dressed group of women at the front of the crowd who had miraculously found a velvet cloak to wrap about her. She was doubly grateful for its warmth as the earl talked on and on. He finally finished by suggesting they sing a hymn and when that was over led the crowd in a rousing chorus of 'God Save the King'. By this time most of the crowd were weeping with emotion.

A garlanded chariot was found and bedecked with ribbons. In it went the mayor, a Mr Dowdy, and his wife with their backs to the horses and Fanny and the earl facing them. There was a scramble and jolting and heaving as the horses were untethered and the crowd proceeded to pull the chariot themselves to the neighboring town while the band went on before, playing, 'See The Conquering Hero Comes.'

Fanny felt exhausted and shattered and buffeted by all the cheering and noise as she had so recently been buffeted by the wind.

'Smile and wave!' hissed the earl in her ear, and so Fanny waved to the cheering crowds, cursing him in her heart for a vain fool.

At the nearby town of Deep they were taken to a posting house and given bedchambers to refresh themselves in and commanded to attend a mayoral banquet that evening while messengers rode to London with the glad news of their safety.

How Fanny got through that terrible evening, she never knew. There were great masses of food and then a personal appearance on the balcony of the town hall and then a fireworks display to attend.

She hated the earl with a black deep hatred. He should have been concerned for her welfare. Had she screamed or fainted or behaved in any missish way? No! But all he did was smile and smile and make those interminable speeches.

It was not until the morning after that they found themselves alone together at last as they set out in a closed carriage on the road to London. The weather had turned wet and blustery, and Fanny was considered too much a heroine to mind the conventions or object to being put in a closed carriage with the earl.

'You, sir,' began Fanny, as soon as the town was left behind, 'are a vain knave and a fool. How you basked in all that adulation. What lies you told those poor people.'

'A little exaggeration, that is all,' said the earl mildly.

'All that business of a ray of light from God pointing the way,' scoffed Fanny.

'Think,' he said. 'Our deliverance was a miracle, whatever way you like to look at it. Did you not mark how poor that village was? Now, for a short time, it will be on the map. People will come from all over to see where Almighty Providence intervened. The shopkeepers of Deep-Under-Lime will make money and so will everyone else. Why deprive people of enjoyment and fun? They have so very little. You were not hurt. If I may say so, you have shown remarkable stamina and look more beautiful than ever.'

'You may have forgotten,' said Fanny in a thin

voice, 'but I am a woman, and yet you showed not a whit of concern for my well-being.'

'I would have shown a great deal of impatience if you had added to my misery by behaving in a hysterical manner. Come now, Miss Fanny, are not you bluestockings always going on about how you are as strong as men?'

'Intellectually, but not physically.'

'Then be grateful for a strong mind that enabled you to bear danger in a commendable way. You cannot have it both ways. If you want me to treat you as I would treat a silly, twittering miss, then you must be silly and twitter and look at me as if I were the most marvelous man in the whole world.'

He smiled in a superior way at Fanny's averted face. Fanny suddenly looked at him with a world of tenderness and adoration in her eyes. Her body appeared to sway toward him, and she said huskily, 'Oh, my hero!'

He was shaken to the core. His hands were about to reach for her when she said maliciously, 'Something like that, my lord?'

'You are a play actress and a minx,' he said furiously. 'You would have me believe that men and women are intellectually equal, and yet that is not so. Women are cruel. They take things too personally, whereas a man is able to dismiss petty slights and insults.'

'Fustian,' said Fanny. 'What actions of female violence at any time ever exceeded the cool determined cruelty of eastern princes who murder all their brethren, on their accession to the throne, from the jealousy of rivalship?'

'Then take vanity. Women are more vain than men,' said the earl, feeling huffy.

'Vanity is not confined to women,' said Fanny. 'Nature has given to man a penetration to discover when he is agreeable to woman, but vanity will not suffer him to discover when he ceases to be so. Men have much more steadiness in hiding their vanity – that is all. Come, sir, I believe any Bond Street fribble could outdo any woman in vanity.'

The earl glared at her. 'You are nothing more than one of those females who dislike men.'

Fanny laughed. 'I have had little opportunity in my life to date to have any acquaintance with men. Only you, my lord, and you must allow me the liberty to dislike or like you as it suits me.'

'I could not have such a conversation with a man,' pointed out the earl.

'Of course you couldn't,' said Fanny. 'Any social equal of yours being patronized in such a way would soon call you out.'

'I am tired,' said the earl abruptly. 'I am going to sleep.'

He closed his eyes.

Fanny glared at him. 'Coward,' she said. But the earl did seem to fall asleep very promptly, leaving Fanny to her thoughts. Those thoughts turned homeward. She hoped the girls and Mrs Waverley had received the news that she was safe.

* * *

They had not.

The mayor's messengers had ridden to the earl's town house and had given the news to his servants, but had not called on Mrs Waverley, assuming that Lord Tredair's household would let that lady know.

Frederica and Felicity cried and cried. Frederica said, between sobs, that she was going to hang herself. She had murdered Fanny, and Felicity did not help by crying and agreeing with every word.

Mrs Waverley sat by the window of the drawing room, her Bible on her lap, looking down into the street. She had remained there the previous night and was still there on the following day.

The candles and lamps had not been lighted, and the house was full of shadows when Frederica followed by Felicity came in and threw herself at Mrs Waverley's feet.

'Now, child,' said Mrs Waverley quietly, 'you must not give way. There is still hope.'

'There is something I have to confess,' sobbed Frederica.

There came the sounds of a carriage rattling over the road outside. Mrs Waverley held up her hand.

'It is of no use. She will not come back,' wailed Frederica. Mrs Waverley threw up the window and then held tightly onto the sill.

'It's Fanny,' she said. 'Oh, dear Fanny,' and moving with remarkable speed for so heavy a woman, she rushed downstairs.

Across the square Lady Artemis was entertaining Mr Fordyce. She was dressed becomingly in transparent black muslin. Mr Fordyce was holding her hand. 'Do not cry, dear Lady Artemis,' he said. 'I cannot be persuaded that Tredair is dead. Amazingly powerful fellow.'

'It is my fault,' said Lady Artemis, who was sitting close beside Mr Fordyce on the sofa. 'I should never have introduced him to those Waverley women.' And her head dropped until it rested on Mr Fordyce's shoulder.

'It was not your fault,' said Mr Fordyce, patting her back and longing for the courage to kiss her. 'Some ruffian cut the ropes of the balloon.'

'Oh, thank you for being so kind,' breathed Lady Artemis, turning a tear-stained face up to his. Her mouth quivered. Demme, I *am* going to kiss her, thought Mr Fordyce. He leaned forward. There came the sound of shrill exclamations and shouts from the square. Lady Artemis ran to the window so suddenly and neatly that he nearly fell on his face.

'It is Tredair!' she cried. 'He is safe!'

The earl helped Fanny out of the carriage and stood smiling as Fanny was kissed and hugged by Frederica and Felicity. He gave Mrs Waverley a brief outline of their adventures, refused any offers of refreshment, but said he would call soon to make sure Miss Fanny had not suffered from her experiences.

He was turning away to get back into the carriage when Lady Artemis came rushing up, hair tumbled and eyes shining. She threw herself against the earl's chest, crying, 'Oh, thank God you are safe. My hero.'

The earl's green eyes flashed a wicked look at

Fanny over Lady Artemis's head, then he gently detached himself.

Mrs Waverley and the girls bore Fanny off into the house. Fanny felt exhausted and depressed. Of course, that sort of silly gushing female was just what men liked.

She pulled herself together and over the tea tray told the girls and Mrs Waverley all about her adventures.

'You are a credit to my training,' said Mrs Waverley. 'His lordship must admire your stamina and courage.'

'I think Lord Tredair would have liked me better if I had screamed and fainted,' said Fanny tartly.

She gradually felt more peaceful. The house was warm and secure. For the first time she began to look forward to the monotony of her days – days free from upsetting and disturbing men.

She was about to rise and go upstairs to her bed-chamber when Mrs Ricketts, the housekeeper, appeared. 'Now that Miss Fanny is safe, mum,' said the housekeeper, 'would you like me to go ahead with the inventory tomorrow?'

'Yes, Ricketts,' said Mrs Waverley. She smiled at the girls. 'We are about to expand our horizons. I feel Lady Artemis has the right of it. There are many women in society who would benefit from our experience. To that end, we shall be entertaining a wider circle. Now, we all have very valuable jewels and it is a sad fact that there are thieves even amongst the highest ranks of society. Have all your jewelry ready for inspection tomorrow. Ricketts will make a note of it and bring it to me. A little precaution, that is all. I am sure I could produce a list from my head. Off to bed, girls. You are all quite white with excitement.'

The three Waverley girls went upstairs and by unspoken accord went into Fanny's bedchamber and shut the door behind them.

'What are we going to do?' said Frederica. 'Will we never be at peace again? First I think I am a murderess, then . . .'

'A murderess!' exclaimed Fanny. 'You cut those ropes! You tried to get me killed. But why?'

'I didn't try to kill you,' said Frederica sulkily. 'Felicity and I thought you were betraying us by getting spoony over Tredair, and we thought it would be fun to tip you out of the basket.'

'I am not in love with Lord Tredair!' howled Fanny.

They all began to shout at once, accusing and protesting. They were so busy arguing, they did not hear the door open. The next thing they knew, Mrs Waverley had crashed into the room and was standing over them, glaring.

'If you behave like naughty children, then you will be treated as such,' said Mrs Waverley furiously. 'To your beds immediately. Bread and water tomorrow and stay in your rooms!'

Later that night Fanny lay awake, still furious with Felicity and Frederica, but wishing she had not been part of such a noisy row.

The door creaked open and Felicity and Frederica crept in.

'Truce,' said Frederica, holding up her hand. 'What are we going to do about these jewels?'

'You see,' said Felicity urgently, 'if she finds out they are missing, then she may blame the servants and that would be awful.'

'Did you never redeem any of them?' asked Fanny. The two girls dismally shook their heads.

'There is only one thing we can do,' said Fanny slowly. 'We must wait until Ricketts completes the inventory, then we must take some more of the jewels and redeem the other ones and then pretend to find them, and then somehow we are going to have to raise money to get *those* jewels back, don't you see? It was wicked of us after all Mrs Waverley's kindness. Do you think, perhaps, our parents were thieves? How odd that none of us know our parents. How odd to think they may have died on the gallows.'

'But how are we to get out tomorrow?' asked Felicity. 'We are confined to our rooms.'

'Mrs Waverley never comes near us when we are in disgrace,' said Fanny. 'I can contrive to escape. Now, what jewels have you pawned and have you the tickets?'

'We have the tickets,' said Felicity. 'We only started about a month ago so there isn't much – a pearl brooch, a garnet necklace, and an amethyst bracelet.'

'I pawned a diamond pin,' said Fanny, 'and I have enough money left to redeem those items. I need only take one thing to redeem the diamond pin.'

They plotted and planned until far into the night.

* * *

Everything went according to plan. The minute Ricketts had completed the inventory, Fanny slipped from the house by way of the library window. She carried in her reticule the pawn tickets and a fine diamond brooch. The pawnbroker was furious. He had been about to sell the items, confident that the mysterious 'Lady Tremblant' would never redeem them. But the diamond brooch she was offering was a choice item, and this time she seemed to be prepared to accept only the same amount she had received for the diamond pin.

Fanny took the redeemed items and fled back. She found someone had removed the plank from the wall of the neighboring house. She had no time to wonder who would do such a thing. She flung herself at the wall and scrabbled up it with such energy that she shot over the top and landed heavily on the other side, not on the rain barrel, but in a clump of bushes beside it.

Once back inside the house, she gave the girls the items and all hid them in unexpected places. Then one by one they summoned Ricketts to explain their 'finds'. The items were duly added to the inventory that was shown to Mrs Waverley who declared it complete.

With a sigh of relief the Waverley girls settled down to the confinement of their rooms and munched dry bread and drank water, all that they were to be allowed.

Downstairs, Mrs Waverley read all the newspapers for about the third time.

All carried exciting accounts of the balloon adventure of Miss Fanny Waverley and Lord Tredair. The authorities were still hunting for the ruffian who had sliced the ropes.

One paper referred to Fanny as a 'golden goddess descending from heaven.' Mrs Waverley's heart swelled with pride. How clever her three girls were. How very beautiful and perfect and so full of grace. Everyone would want to meet Fanny. For a moment Mrs Waverley's pleasure was dimmed at the thought of letting intrusive society into the safety of her home. But it was unthinkable that such a triumph should go uncelebrated. Of course, if Fanny had formed a tendre for Lord Tredair, that would be awkward. Fanny must be brought to realize she had no hopes in that direction. An earl would not marry a girl from the orphanage who did not know the identity of her parents. And he would surely find out, because if there was even the hint of a marriage, his family and lawyers would ferret out Fanny's background. 'And my own!' thought Mrs Waverley in sudden dismay.

A little taste of the world for the girls and then they must retire back into their usual seclusion and be persuaded to give up any dreams of marriage.

A downstairs maid, Betty, announced the arrival of the Earl of Tredair. Mrs Waverley at first decided to tell him the girls were confined to their rooms and then just as he entered, thought better of it. The girls were not expecting to be allowed out of their rooms and would be in their oldest clothes.

She waited until the earl was seated and murmuring an apology went out onto the landing and told Betty to bring the young misses down to the drawing room, but not to tell them there was a visitor.

Fanny, Felicity, and Frederica were relieved when they got the summons. Mrs Waverley must have forgiven them. The three were wearing loose drab gowns, the ones they wore under their cloaks when they went out walking.

The earl was standing by the fireplace as they entered. He found it very hard not to stare at Fanny. He had thought of her frequently as she had looked in that naughty, flimsy gown with her gold hair spilling about her shoulders. That gold hair was now screwed up on top of her head in a hard knot, and she and the other two girls looked like schoolgirls from one of the less expensive Bath seminaries.

'My dear Miss Fanny,' he said, taking her hand and kissing the air somewhere above it, 'what has happened to you? You appear somewhat distrait.'

'It must be the effect of my adventures. I am not made of iron, my lord,' said Fanny, tugging her hand away and averting her face.

'And you have twigs in your hair.'

'It's a very interesting fashion, my lord,' said Frederica desperately. She and Felicity had heard of Fanny's fall into the bush and had been trying to help her get the twigs and leaves out when they were summoned. 'We read about a new way of curling the hair by twisting it around twigs. We were trying it out on Fanny when we were summoned here, and I am afraid we had not time to get them all out. Is that not so, Felicity?'

'Oh, definitely,' agreed that young lady cheerfully.

'Lady Artemis Verity,' announced Mrs Ricketts dolefully. Lady Artemis came tripping in, wrapped in a cloud of scent and gauze shawls. She affected a start of surprise when she saw the earl, but in fact had espied his arrival at the Waverleys through her telescope.

She curtsied to Mrs Waverley and then turned to Fanny, her eyes widening in delight when she saw the drabness of her appearance.

A look of hellish glee in his eyes, the earl said to Fanny, 'You must explain to Lady Artemis this exciting fashion of wearing twigs in the hair.'

Frederica weighed into the rescue again. 'Yes, 'tis a most novel idea, Lady Artemis. I believe the women of the Indian tribes in Virginia use such a method. I . . .'

'I fear my silly girls are talking rubbish,' interrupted Mrs Waverley. 'Life is so difficult sometimes trying to keep them in order. They are little more than schoolgirls and behave as such. I found them shouting and screaming at each other last night and had to punish the naughty little things by keeping them locked in their rooms.'

Lady Artemis let out a little trill of laughter. Fanny looked at the elegance of her gown, the beauty of her clear complexion, the sophisticated and seductive movements of her body, and decided all in that moment she hated Lady Artemis with a passion.

She also felt a stab of hate for Mrs Waverley. She was deliberately going out of her way to make them appear like spoiled schoolgirls in front of the earl. In the past Mrs Waverley had always seemed amused by their quarrels, often, Fanny now realized with a sense of shock, going out of her way to set one against the other. Her soft lips formed into a hard line.

'I fear you must find us very badly brought up, Lady Artemis. But, as you know, we have not been allowed to go in the company of civilized people.' Mrs Waverley glared and bridled.

'But that is why I have come,' cried Lady Artemis. 'I am giving a little party for a few friends, all of them agog to meet the . . . er . . . beautiful Miss Fanny and hear of her adventures. You, too, must attend, my lord. An impromptu affair tomorrow night, for as you know we were all to attend the Petershams' rout, and they have cried off at the very last moment, Mrs Petersham having the migraine.'

The earl did not want to attend. London had again lost all interest for him. He wanted to return to the peace of the country. But he could not quite think how to refuse, so he bowed and said he would be charmed. Mrs Waverley, furious with Fanny, decided to accept. Fanny deserved to be humiliated further for having told Lady Artemis her upbringing had been somewhat short of the best.

The earl took his leave. Lady Artemis left with him. She looked quite radiant. 'What frumpy gowns those poor girls do insist on wearing,' she said, smiling up into the earl's eyes.

'They have great intelligence and animation,' he said, feeling defensive and wondering why at the same time, 'and are suffering from their odd teaching.'

The smile left Lady Artemis's face. 'May I persuade you to take tea with me, my lord?'

'Your servant, ma'am,' he said, bowing low, 'but I have a pressing engagement.'

He raised his hat and walked away, oblivious to the pout on Lady Artemis's lips.

FIVE

Fanny called the girls into her room that evening. She was shocked and worried. Mrs Waverley had taught them to be proud of their intelligence and looks. Now they had all been exposed as badly behaved and spoiled creatures with neither breeding nor wit.

'What do you want to see us about?' asked Frederica.

'I am ashamed of us all,' said Fanny in a low voice. 'What a sorry threesome Mrs Waverley contrived to make us look today!'

'Oh, that,' shrugged Felicity. 'You are just mad because your handsome lord saw you looking drab and obviously prefers the charms of Lady Artemis.'

For one brief moment Fanny felt like shouting at her sisters again.

'I am angry because I feel we have been manipulated into disliking each other by Mrs Waverley,' she said.

'We scrap and row but we don't hate each other, do we?' asked Frederica.

'There were times when I hated you,' said Fanny in a low voice.

'Why?'

'You told Mrs Waverley that my looks were blousy and insipid, that my coloring made me look like a milkmaid.'

'I never did!' gasped Frederica.

'And you, Felicity, you said to Mrs Waverley that I was possessed of a good memory, but had no real intelligence.'

'Never!'

'And a score of other nasty things,' pursued Fanny.

'But *you* told her you often thought my parents must have been gypsies,' exclaimed Frederica. 'You told Mrs Waverley there was a certain peasant wildness about me.'

'And that time I got up in the night and stole that cake from the kitchen,' said Felicity. 'I shared it with you, Fanny, and yet you went and told her about it the very next morning.'

'On my oath, I never said or did any of those things,' said Fanny. 'Don't you see what has been happening? I felt bound close to Mrs Waverley, for I felt I could not confide in you or trust you. I felt you were being nice to my face and saying awful things about me behind my back.'

'If this is true,' said Frederica slowly, 'then Mrs Waverley is a very wicked woman.'

'No, not wicked,' said Fanny. 'I think she is a coward. She seems frightened to go out of the house. Only look at our strange life. Who *is* Mrs Waverley? Have you thought of that? Who was Mr Waverley? Where does the money come from?'

'I never thought of it,' said Felicity, running her fingers nervously through her chestnut hair. 'I was always so taken up with wondering who *we* were and where we came from. We cannot have had low parents, for the orphanage was very genteel and in a lower one we would already have been found posts as servants. But Mrs Waverley made our incarceration here seem so logical. It is a man's world, and she made us feel like a courageous band of women who had decided to live their own lives. I cannot find fault with her ideas, you know. Women do not have any rights to speak of. What is marriage? Tied to some tyrant for life and only allowed peace after one has produced a string of babies and miscarriages.'

Frederica looked slyly at Fanny. 'But what if one falls in love with a handsome man like, say, the Earl of Tredair?'

Fanny had a brief thought of what it would be like to be shackled to the Earl of Tredair for life. The idea that it might be heaven came to her, and she decided her nerves must be sadly overwrought.

'Stop teasing me about the Earl of Tredair,' she snapped. 'We should study these members of society at Lady Artemis's party and watch how they go on.

On the other hand, it is all very well to have high principles but I, for one, do not want to appear as a sort of sideshow to amuse Lady Artemis's guests. Believe me, Lady Artemis will make a great story out of our quarrel and how Mrs Waverley locked us in our rooms. We shall be treated with contempt.'

'We could all fall ill,' said Frederica, after a long silence.

'Mrs Waverley would send for the doctor and he would soon find out we were malingering,' jeered Felicity.

'Wait a bit.' Fanny sat up straight. 'Dr MacAllister is short-sighted. He is also morbidly afraid of catching an infection himself. If we were to paint red spots on our faces, he would stand at the end of the bed and not dare to come any nearer. Fetch your paint-box, Felicity. We have work to do!'

Lady Artemis was furious. Her drawing room was crowded with the cream of the ton. The earl and Mr Fordyce were there as was Lord Alvanley, Lord Petersham, Lord Byron and many more fascinating and interesting men, not to mention some high-nosed ladies who had been chosen for their social position rather than their looks. Lady Artemis did not want any competition. Not only did Lady Artemis feel she had brought them all to her house on false pretences, but she considered it outrageous that Mrs Waverley should come alone from an infected house. Lady Artemis kept stealing looks at herself every time she passed a looking glass as if dreading to see red spots beginning to pop out all over her face.

'You must be relieved that the ladies are ill,' said Mr Fordyce to the earl. 'You appear to have taken the beautiful Miss Fanny in dislike.'

'Not I,' said the earl. 'I was simply angry at having allowed myself to be coerced into attending this tedious affair.'

He would not confess to himself that he was disappointed. He tried to remember Fanny with that awful hairstyle and dowdy gown, but all he could remember was all that glorious fall of golden hair and how soft and pliant her body had felt against his in the balloon.

'Now Lady Artemis is in the suds,' he said.

'Why?' asked Mr Fordyce.

'Well, from the cheers outside and the commotion downstairs, I fear Prinny himself has arrived to see the latest heroine.'

Sure enough, the Prince Regent was announced. Lady Artemis fluttered across to welcome him, explaining nervously that Miss Fanny and her sisters had been struck down by a mysterious affliction.

The royal eye fell on the earl, and the portly royal figure moved toward him. 'Tell me of your adventures, Tredair,' said the prince.

The earl obliged, giving almost as highly colored an account as he had given the villagers of Deep-Under-Lime. The prince was obviously enjoying himself and Lady Artemis began to relax. The earl finished his story and then said, 'But, sire, although Miss Fanny is not present, Mrs Waverley is.'

'Ah, yes, the gel's mother,' said the prince. 'Which is she?'

Lord Tredair did not think it necessary to point out that Mrs Waverley was not Fanny's mother. Instead he nodded across the room and said, 'The lady yonder in the purple turban.'

The Prince Regent raised his quizzing glass, looked at Mrs Waverley, and muttered, 'It can't be.'

'I beg your pardon, sire,' said the earl.

'Nothing . . . nothing. Must leave. Pressing engagements, lots to do.'

The earl watched curiously as the prince walked across the room to take his leave. Then the prince stopped as he came abreast of Mrs Waverley. That lady's face had lost all color. She curtsied low. The earl went and stood behind the prince. 'Clorinda?' said the prince, his voice barely above a whisper. 'Can it be you?'

Mrs Waverley gave him a look of mute appeal and then quickly dropped her eyes. 'Charmed to meet you,' said the prince in a loud voice. 'Sorry your daughter is indisposed. Brave lady. Good day to you all.'

The earl tried to engage Mrs Waverley in conversation, but she was trembling and abstracted. Had it not been for that overheard whisper of 'Clorinda', the earl would have assumed she was overcome simply by the honor of meeting the Prince Regent. At last, in great agitation, she protested she felt faint, strongly refused his offer to escort her home, and took her leave.

'I think we should go as well,' said the earl, return-
ing to Mr Fordyce.

'We've only just got here!' cried Mr Fordyce, looking longingly in the direction of Lady Artemis.

'Stay by all means,' said the earl. 'I shall most probably see you at the club later.'

But he spoke to thin air. Lady Artemis had just
smiled in their direction and Mr Fordyce had
assumed that smile to be for himself and was now
standing beside her, talking earnestly.

The earl hesitated before leaving Hanover Square.
It would do no harm, surely, to call and pay his
respects to Mrs Waverley. He had not asked her
about Fanny.

But when he knocked at the Waverley mansion,
Mrs Ricketts, after leaving him standing in the hall
for what seemed a very long time, returned to tell
him that now Mrs Waverley, too, was indisposed and
would not be receiving visitors for some time.

By the next day the Waverley girls had washed
off their spots and were prepared to venture once
more into the outside world. But it transpired that
even their walks in the square were canceled. Mrs
Waverley kept to her rooms and refused to see them
or anyone. After four days of this gloom, the rebel-
lious Frederica put on her bonnet and cloak and
made to leave the house to take a walk, only to find
her way barred by Mrs Ricketts and two maids. No
one was to leave the house, said Mrs Ricketts sourly,
and force was to be used if necessary.

Bewildered, Frederica returned to tell the others. 'Then we'll need to use the library window again,' said Felicity. 'Me first. I feel if I do not get out of here, I shall scream. Have you any money, Fanny?'

'I have quite a lot left over from pawning that brooch,' said Fanny, 'but I meant to keep it until we could raise some more money to add to it and get the trinket back.'

'Just a little bit,' pleaded Felicity. 'Just enough to buy a trifle in one of the shops.'

Fanny relented. She was enjoying their new found friendship and closeness and did not want to spoil it.

So Felicity went out that day, and Frederica the next. Fanny could hardly wait for it to be her turn. The silence in the house was oppressive. Mrs Waverley still refused to see anyone, although people knocked at the door all day long. Everyone was anxious to meet Fanny, who had featured so largely in the newspapers.

'So you have decided to set yourself up in style,' said the earl to Mr Fordyce as they walked through the elegant streets of the West End.

'Yes, it seems silly to live in cramped lodgings when I have the ready to hire a town house,' said Mr Fordyce. 'Barton told me he'd got a place to rent, and you'll never guess where it is.'

'Where?'

'Right slap bang next to Mrs Waverley,' said Mr Fordyce.

'And right across the square from Lady Artemis,' said the earl slyly.

Mr Fordyce blushed. 'Coincidence, that's all,' he muttered. 'I mean, it's demned difficult to find a place during the Season. Barton is asking a reasonable rent.'

'Don't make up your mind until you see the place,' cautioned the earl. 'He may be asking a reasonable rent because it's ready to fall down.'

'I'm on my way there,' said Mr Fordyce. 'Come and see it with me. You can call on the Waverleys.'

'I have no interest in the Waverleys,' said the earl. 'In fact, I do not have much interest in anything at the Season.'

'Then why attend?'

'I do hope to get married one day. I am getting somewhat long in the tooth.'

'Should be easy for *you*,' said Mr Fordyce, jealously. 'You have only to drop the handkerchief.'

'Ah, but I think marriage should involve companionship, and I have not yet met a lady who would not bore me after a very short time.' For some reason he felt a sudden stab of disloyalty to Fanny. Absence from her was blurring that dowdy image of drab clothes and twig strewn hair.

'I should think any man would be fascinated by Lady Artemis for life.'

'Ah, but I am a difficult creature. I wish you well.'

'I do not think I have much hope there,' said Mr Fordyce wistfully. 'She won't even look at me when you're in the room. I thought she was smiling at me at her party, but when I went to join her, all she could do was exclaim at you taking your leave so early and say how disappointed she was and ask me all sorts of things about you.'

'Persevere,' said the earl cheerfully. 'They often pretend to be interested in your friend when they are interested in you.'

'I wish I believed that,' said Mr Fordyce. 'I shall be in a good position to plan a campaign if this house is at all bearable.'

They made their way toward the tall house adjoining the Waverley mansion.

Mr Fordyce fished in his pocket and produced an enormous key.

The door creaked open and they walked into a large hall. The house was double fronted with a saloon, a morning room, and a library on the ground floor. On the first floor was a large drawing room, dining room, study, and another saloon. Above that were the bedrooms.

Everything smelled damp and dusty. Mr Fordyce got down on his hands and knees and poked up the drawing room chimney with his cane and then leapt back as a cascade of soot tumbled down the chimney. 'All the chimneys need sweeping, I'll bet,' he said gloomily.

'And everything needs scrubbing. Let's go up and examine the beds,' said the earl. 'Bound to be lumpy.'

The beds were, as the earl had feared, lumpy. But Mr Fordyce, glancing out of one of the bedroom windows, saw Lady Artemis driving out in her carriage, and his mood changed.

'I think the house is splendid,' he cried. 'Just a little

cleaning and scrubbing and firing and it will be as right as rain.'

'Do you really need all this?' asked the earl, shaking the bed hangings and releasing a choking cloud of dust.

'I plan to entertain, and I cannot entertain in lodgings.'

'Well, if you'll take my advice, you'll offer that old screw, Barton, half of whatever he demanded.'

'I'll try. Anyway, we've seen everything.'

'No, we haven't,' said the earl. 'You'd better have a look at the kitchen.'

Mr Fordyce surveyed his tall friend in amazement. 'Kitchens? Why?'

'My very dear friend, if you want to keep a good chef, you have to have a suitable place to house him. Kitchens are very important.'

'Oh, very well,' said Mr Fordyce reluctantly.

They made their way down to the basement, and the earl pushed open a door and revealed a large, gloomy kitchen. It was a typical kitchen of the times, except that it was rank and dirty. The walls, which should have been limewashed two or three times a year, were black with smoke and grease, and the floor, which should have been sluiced and scrubbed daily, was slippery with dirt. There was an open fire and a spit.

'You see how important it is to examine the kitchen?' said the earl. 'Any chef or housekeeper would faint if they saw this. You need a squad of scrubbing women and then you need men to limewash the walls. You'll have to install one of these new kitcheners. Everyone uses cooking stoves now. Just look at those pots! Throw the lot out and buy new ones. I say, do you really want to go through all this? You can use my house to entertain, if you wish.'

'You won't recognize the place by the time I'm finished with it,' said Mr Fordyce with a cheerfulness he did not feel.

'Let's see what else there is,' said the earl, leading the way. 'Servants hall, dark and poky, and dirty like all the rest. Still room, store room, preserving room. I suppose there is a garden of sorts?' He unlocked the back door and tugged it hard. It was stuck fast with the damp. He put his booted foot against the wall and wrenched hard. The door sprang open to reveal a weedy garden beyond.

'I don't see why these London gardens should be so neglected,' said the earl crossly. 'There are plenty of bushes that will survive the constant rain of London soot. And . . .'

He stopped talking suddenly and cocked his head to one side. There came a scrabbling sound from the other side of the wall.

Both men turned and looked at the wall that separated the garden from that of Mrs Waverley's. As they watched, the top of a bonnet appeared over the edge of the wall to be followed by the determined face of Miss Fanny Waverley. She was so intent on her escape that she did not notice the two men. She sat astride the plank, which one of the girls must have found, and propped again on Mr Fordyce's side of the wall, slid down, then stood up, and brushed down her skirts.

'Good afternoon, Miss Fanny,' said the earl.

Fanny started and blushed. 'Oh, don't tell on me,' she cried impulsively. 'I have to escape.'

'Escape? Why?' asked the earl.

'We are not allowed out,' said Fanny wretchedly. 'Not even for a walk in the square. So we have been in the way of escaping by this route, just to walk about the streets and parks for a little.'

'Is Mrs Waverley still indisposed?'

'I do not think there is anything very much up with her,' said Fanny. 'It all happened after she had been to that party at Lady Artemis's. She returned home and locked herself up in her rooms and gave instructions that we were not to be allowed out. What are you doing here?'

'Mr Fordyce is going to rent this house.'

'Oh.' Fanny's face fell. 'Now what are we to do?'

'It does seem hard,' said Mr Fordyce, 'that you should not be allowed out. I tell you what, Miss Fanny, I shall pretend I do not see any of you, and you may still use this route.'

'But you will have servants,' said Fanny. 'And they will talk to *our* servants and that will be an end of it.'

'Are you recovered from your illness?' asked the earl.

'What illness?' asked Fanny and then blushed again and looked at the ground. 'Oh, *that* illness. Yes, thank you, my lord. I am recovered.'

'Tell me, Miss Fanny, why did you really have twigs in your hair?'

'I was getting over the wall and fell into the bushes.'

'So that explains it. Does Mrs Waverley know the Prince Regent?' asked the earl abruptly. Fanny's eyes flew to meet his. 'Of course not. She would have said so. Who would not?'

'I thought I overheard him say, "Clorinda" to her at Lady Artemis's party.'

'You must be mistaken,' said Fanny. 'Her name is Maria. But the Prince Regent was there! Oh, wait until I tell the girls. They will be disappointed not to have met him.'

'I think the whole of society is disappointed at not meeting *you*, Miss Fanny. One after the other tells me of calls on your house.'

Fanny shrugged slightly. 'They have already ceased to call. I am no longer a celebrity. Are you really going to take this house, Mr Fordyce? It looks sadly neglected from the outside.'

'And hideously neglected on the inside. But nothing will deter Mr Fordyce. How did you plan to get around the front?' asked the earl.

'There is a path there that leads around the side of the house and up the area steps,' said Fanny. 'Perhaps I should not go. I am always afraid of discovery.'

'It is monstrous you should be so cooped up,' said Mr Fordyce, his kind heart touched. 'Perhaps Lady Artemis has some influence with Mrs Waverley and can persuade her to take you about.'

'Mrs Waverley will see no one, not even Lady

Artemis,' said Fanny. She stopped and listened. 'Oh, dear, our servants have finished their tea and are back in the kitchens. I am always afraid they will see me when I return.'

'Come and see my new abode,' said Mr Fordyce expansively, 'and then we may hit upon a way to get you back in your own front door.'

Fanny followed them into the house. She was relieved that the presence of the earl was not disturbing her. No suffocating heartbeats, no trembling knees. She exclaimed at the mess that was the kitchen.

'Mrs Waverley would be shocked,' she said. 'She has very strong views on kitchens. Ours has the latest in closed stoves and is always clean and sparkling. And the kitchen servants have real beds and are not made to sleep on the floor in front of the kitchen fire as they are in most households.'

'Would she feel strongly about this kitchen?' asked the earl curiously.

Fanny looked at him in surprise, and then laughed. 'She would be itching to manage the whole thing and Mr Fordyce as well.'

'Then perhaps this is just the tonic she needs,' said the earl. 'Follow me, Miss Fanny, I have a plan.'

The earl knocked at the door of Mrs Waverley's mansion. Mr Fordyce stood behind him. Mrs Ricketts answered the door.

'Come with me, Mrs Ricketts,' commanded the earl. 'I wish to show you something.'

The housekeeper bobbed a curtsy and followed him next door. The earl pointed down into the area.

'Mr Fordyce is going to rent this place, but the kitchen is a disgrace. Do you think Mrs Waverley would be interested in letting Mr Fordyce have the benefit of her advice? It sadly needs a woman's touch.' As Mrs Ricketts leaned over the railings, the earl glanced sideways and saw out of the corner of his eye Fanny slipping in through the street door that Mrs Ricketts had left standing open.

'Very particular about kitchens is Mrs Waverley,' said Mrs Ricketts. 'And the poor lady does need an interest, she's been that low recently. But she won't see anyone.'

'Perhaps if you could furnish me with pen and paper,' said the earl, 'I could persuade her.'

'You can try, my lord,' said Mrs Ricketts, 'but I don't know that it will do any good.'

The earl and Mr Fordyce followed Mrs Ricketts back indoors. She led them to the library and indicated a desk over against one wall.

The earl took out his penknife and sharpened a quill and then looked thoughtfully at the paper. That little whisper of the Prince Regent's of 'Clorinda' still nagged. Had she gone into hiding for fear of seeing him again? Then he wrote, 'Dear Mrs Waverley, Mr Fordyce is desirous of renting the property next door, but the kitchen is in a sad mess and he is in need of help and advice. He has not followed the Prince Regent to Brighton, but has decided to try to enjoy the rest of the Season in more commodious accommodation. We are waiting below and should both be immensely grateful if you could spare us a few moments of your valuable time. Your humble and obedient servant, Tredair.'

'What's all that about Brighton?' asked Mr Fordyce, peering over the earl's shoulder. 'I had no intention of going to that watering place, prince or no prince.'

'Hush,' said the earl, sanding the letter and handing it to Mrs Ricketts.

Mrs Waverley was lying on a day bed by the window of her bedchamber when Mrs Ricketts entered with the earl's letter. She had lost weight and there were pouches under her eyes.

'What is it, Ricketts?' she asked feebly.

'It's that Earl of Tredair,' said Mrs Ricketts.

'Send him away.'

'Yes, mum, but you'd best give me an answer to his letter.'

'Oh, very well.' Mrs Waverley read the letter and then read it again. Her eyebrows rose in surprise. A faint tinge of color appeared in her cheeks. 'What an odd request!' she exclaimed. 'And yet, men are so helpless. If the management of parliament was left to women, you would see a change for the better, Ricketts.'

'Yes, mum,' said Mrs Ricketts, beginning to smile. A Mrs Waverley on the subject of the superiority of women was a Mrs Waverley beginning to recover. 'Won't you see them? I've put them in the library. Ever so upset his lordship was about his friend's kitchen. Really dirty he said it was.'

Mrs Waverley flung back the rug that covered her and rose majestically, the light of battle in her eyes. 'Go ahead, Ricketts,' she said. 'I will see them myself.'

In ten minutes time Mrs Waverley was standing in the filthy kitchen next door, looking about her cheerfully.

'I suggest you leave the management of this to me, Mr Fordyce. Men are so weak and helpless when it comes to management. Ricketts! Fetch the girls and tell them to put on their old clothes and aprons. Bring the other servants. Let battle commence!'

'I say, ma'am,' said Mr Fordyce, round-eyed, as Mrs Waverley began to roll up her sleeves. 'You're never going to tackle this yourself. Not to mention your girls!'

'A lady should be able to do anything a servant can do and better!' said Mrs Waverley.

'And a gentleman,' said the earl, removing his coat and beginning to roll up his sleeves as well. 'With your permission, ma'am, I shall go next door and help the girls carry all the cleaning tools.'

Lady Artemis returned from her drive and as usual went up to her drawing room and peered through her telescope at the Waverley mansion, hoping for a glimpse of the Earl of Tredair.

All of a sudden he came into focus, walking into that house next door with those Waverley girls and all of them carrying mops and pails and brushes. The earl was in his shirt sleeves and was laughing at something Frederica was saying. Fanny looked flushed and excited and her hair gleamed like pale gold.

Screaming for her lady's maid, Lady Artemis erupted into her bedchamber, scrabbling in her wardrobe for her oldest clothes.

When she considered she was suitably dressed, she hurried over the square and made her way down the area steps where she had seen the party descending.

The Waverley girls were scrubbing down the walls, the earl was down on his hands and knees scrubbing the floor, Mrs Waverley was through in the scullery, rattling pots and pans, Mr Fordyce was standing helplessly in the middle of the kitchen, and the Waverley servants were working on the servants hall, the still room, and the storage room.

'It's a cleaning party,' said the earl. 'Mr Fordyce *will* insist on living here, and Mrs Waverley is giving us all a lesson in housewifery.'

Lady Artemis looked into his laughing, mocking, tantalizing green eyes.

She carefully drew off her gloves.

'What a good idea,' she said faintly. 'Where do I start?'

SIX

Lady Artemis dressed to go out that evening with less than her usual care. She was turning over the day's events in her mind. She had only started to clean that disgusting kitchen because the earl was doing so and planned to plead the headache at the first possible opportunity. But, somehow, all the laughter and housework and chatter became enjoyable. Soon the compulsion to have the kitchen shining gripped everyone, including Mr Fordyce. How they had worked! How exciting it had been to see the lime-wash mixed with blue covering the scrubbed walls and to see the copper pans gleaming on the shelves. But more than anything had been the look in the earl's eyes, and his words to her as she had left – 'You are a most fascinating and surprising woman, Lady Artemis.'

The conversation that day had been stimulating as

well. Mrs Waverley had brought up the subject of the masses of prostitutes who thronged the playhouse. At first Lady Artemis had been shocked. One knew that such creatures existed, but one did not talk about them. Mr Fordyce had claimed that all such women were depraved, but Mrs Waverley argued that a great many were forced into prostitution through lack of money, rather than because they were evil. 'Most women,' Mrs Waverley had said, waving a rolling pin to emphasize her point, 'are not, like aristocrats, protected by any marriage settlements. If they are divorced, or if the husband drinks himself to death, they must look about for a way to stop themselves from starving. And what else is there but prostitution? And look at all the jobs held by men that should be performed by women – men-milliners, men-mantua makers, and men-staymakers to mention just a few. Have you read *A Vindication of the Rights of Woman*, by Mary Wollstonecraft, my lord?' To Lady Artemis's amazement, the earl had replied, 'yes,' and had gone on to argue that somehow Mrs Wollstonecraft had, in his opinion, failed to define emancipation or set out the rights women should share.

During the following discussion, names like Mrs Barbauld, Maria Edgeworth, Catharine Macaulay, and Elizabeth Carter had been thrown about. Lady Artemis felt sadly ignorant. She now tried to tell herself that it was not very feminine to argue so much with gentlemen, but the earl had seemed to enjoy it all.

She was still preoccupied with her thoughts when she reached Lord Tomley's, where a ball was being held. So preoccupied was she that she failed to remember that the Tomleys were old-fashioned and kept old-fashioned rules of etiquette. There were no dance cards. Any lady who refused to dance with a gentleman must refuse to dance with all. And so when Lady Artemis looked up and found herself being requested to grant the honor of the first dance to that infernal bore, Colonel Pargeter, she said, 'I am afraid I cannot dance, sir. I am a trifle faint.'

The colonel bristled with anger and stalked away. 'But you love dancing,' exclaimed Miss Follity-Benson, who was sitting next to Lady Artemis. 'What are you going to do? You know you cannot dance with anyone else.'

Lady Artemis bit her lip in vexation. She had forgotten the rules. 'It is not fair,' she said hotly. 'Why should we ladies not be allowed to refuse to dance with men we dislike? Colonel Pargeter squeezes my hand and ogles me dreadfully, and his breath smells like the Serpentine on a hot day with a dead cat floating in it.'

'Well, it does seem hard,' said Miss Follity-Benson, round-eyed, 'but you see, I cannot be so nice in my tastes, for I am very lucky to have any partners at all!'

'Think on it,' went on Lady Artemis, pursuing her theme, 'Look at the way they strut up and down, eyeing us as if we were cattle up for auction at Smithfield. We should have the same rights.'

'We're all at the Season because we need to get married,' said the ever-practical Miss Follity-Benson.

'Not all,' said Lady Artemis. 'You are rich and I am rich and what on earth are we about to sit here meekly waiting to hand our fortunes over to some lout? I tell you, my views have changed since I met Mrs Waverley. She is the mother of that female who was taken up in the balloon. She has been educating me in mathematics and already my household expenses have been cut in half. The tricks servants play! I find knowledge exhilarating. Let me tell you what I have been doing this day.'

The dance had commenced. Several of the wall-flowers drew their chairs around Lady Artemis and listened in amazement as she talked of scrubbing the kitchen. They had more reason to fear the rule of men than Lady Artemis, for they were plain and often ignored at balls, but had never considered anything odd in meekly waiting for a suitor.

Dances ended and dances began and still Lady Artemis talked and talked to her growing court.

Then at one point she looked up and found Mr Fordyce hovering at the edge of the circle. 'Mr Fordyce,' cried Lady Artemis. 'Is Tredair with you?'

'No, my lady,' said Mr Fordyce. 'But I hope you will do me the honor of dancing with me.'

Lady Artemis smiled, rose, and shook out her skirts. 'I should be delighted,' she said.

'The Tomleys will be furious,' hissed Miss Follity-Benson. 'You will not be asked again!'

'Pooh!' said Lady Artemis over her shoulder and then she walked onto the floor with Mr Fordyce.

* * *

That evening Mrs Waverley summoned Fanny to her room. She had noticed the new closeness among the three girls, a closeness from which she felt excluded.

'Sit down, Fanny,' she said. 'I have something to say to you.'

Mrs Waverley surveyed Fanny with pride. The girl really was extraordinarily beautiful with her silver fair hair and deep blue eyes.

'Fanny,' began Mrs Waverley, 'I have a confession to make.'

'Yes, Mrs Waverley?'

'I am not much given to demonstrations of affection, but I would have you know, that of my three charges, I love you the most.'

Fanny squirmed in her chair. She felt she had grown up very recently. Only a short time ago her heart would have been warmed by such a statement. Now she felt she knew the reason. Mrs Waverley was trying to break up their new friendship so as to tie the girls closer to her. She would no doubt summon the other two to tell them the same thing.

'Thank you,' she said, lowering her eyes so that Mrs Waverley should not see the distrust in them.

'You are happy here with me, are you not?' asked Mrs Waverley. Fanny looked up. Mrs Waverley was in her undress. She was wearing a voluminous nightgown, a negligee, and a large muslin cap. She had large pale eyes and a curved nose set in fleshy cheeks and a small mouth. She looked a plump and secure matron. But there was a certain pleading look in her eyes that made Fanny say quickly, 'Of course I am happy, and I am always grateful to you for taking me out of that orphanage. Are you sure, dear Mrs Waverley, that no one knows the identity of my parents?'

Mrs Waverley shook her head, 'As I told you, Fanny, you were a foundling.'

Fanny wrinkled her brow. 'But, you know, I have been thinking, ma'am, that the Pevensey Orphanage only houses young ladies, and although the treatment was harsh, we were at least fed, which, I believe, is more than can be said for most orphanages. Someone must have paid to put me there.'

'That would seem to be the case,' said Mrs Waverley, 'and yet they assured me that the three of you were charity cases. They occasionally swell their ranks by allowing in unfortunates of doubtful birth.'

Fanny flushed miserably.

'Which brings me to Lord Tredair. He is rich and titled and can marry anyone he likes. But a gentleman such as he never stoops so low to marry such as you. I believe him to be mildly interested in you. Pray do not encourage that interest, Fanny, for it means he will offer you a position as his mistress. You would be happy for a while and then he would tire of you, as they all tire sooner or later, and you would be passed on to one of his friends and so it would go on. I have brought you up to be independent of men. Your sad circumstances do not allow you to marry. I am here to protect you from that harsh world of men. Better a celibate spinster life with me than to be the mistress of some man.

'Now, he asked me this afternoon for permission to take you driving in the Park tomorrow. I refused. He taxed me with eccentricity and said that I was bringing you up, not to share the rights of men, but to be afraid of them. In a moment of weakness I gave my permission.' Fanny brightened.

'But you must promise me that you will do or say nothing to attach his affections – affections which will subsequently destroy you.'

'I promise,' said Fanny, who would have promised anything in order to be allowed to drive in the Park at the fashionable hour.

'Thank you,' said Mrs Waverley. 'Always remember you are the one most dear to my heart, Fanny.'

Fanny rose to go.

She looked down curiously at Mrs Waverley. 'Were you not happy in your marriage, ma'am?'

Mrs Waverley's face took on a closed and shuttered look. 'I never talk about it or think about it,' she said firmly.

Fanny left and went to her own room. Soon, she could hear Mrs Ricketts scratching at the door of Frederica's room and her voice telling Frederica that the mistress wanted to see her.

'No doubt she is telling Frederica that *she* is the most loved,' thought Fanny cynically. 'Then she will tell the same thing to Felicity in the hope of making us all jealous of each other again.'

After some time Fanny heard Frederica return and then Mrs Ricketts summoning Felicity.

Fanny waited again until she heard Felicity come

back and then she went to Frederica's room and took her over to Felicity's.

'Did she tell you she loved you more than the rest?' demanded Fanny.

Frederica and Felicity looked at her in amazement and both said, 'yes' in unison.

'Don't you see,' cried Fanny, 'she is trying to set us against each other.'

'Then we shall all go to her room together and tell her we are wise to her,' said Frederica.

'No,' said Fanny. 'That would not answer. We are sorely dependent on her continuing affection.' Only such a short time ago they had been warring schoolgirls. Now three young ladies sat and looked at each other in consternation.

'She has given Lord Tredair permission to take me for a drive in the Park tomorrow,' said Fanny. 'But she told me that I must not encourage him in any way.'

'And neither you should!' said Frederica. 'We are unmarriageable and must stick together.'

'As to the unmarriageable bit,' said Fanny thoughtfully, 'I pointed out to her that someone surely must have been paying to keep me at that orphanage, but she told me we were all charity cases. Now, my dears, just think of that board of governors – the chairman, Mr Wilks, then the director Mrs Goern, and then the others. Can you imagine one of them finding one spark of charity in their flinty hearts? We were fed, yes, but such food! And do you remember on the days when some of the other girls had relatives on a visit, how the food became almost lavish? I am sure the board was taking the money and feeding us slops and pocketing the difference. Such as they would not take on orphans without relatives to pay.'

'I often wonder,' said Felicity sadly, 'who our parents were. But I had come to believe they were disgraceful and probably not even married, so I considered it best not to inquire too closely.'

Fanny lay back on Felicity's bed and clasped her hands behind her head. 'I would like to go back to the orphanage and ask a few questions,' she said dreamily.

'But we cannot,' exclaimed Felicity. 'It is at least an hour's drive and any one of us staying away that long – say we could even find a hack to take us that far – would be missed. An hour there, say half an hour at the orphanage, an hour back – too long.'

'I am going to do it somehow,' said Fanny. 'In the meantime I suggest we continue to play Mrs Waverley's game. An occasional quarrel will keep her happy.'

A tear rolled down Frederica's cheek. 'It does seem hard,' she said in a stifled voice, 'to be in London at the Season and to see young misses going out to balls and parties night after night while we stay in here. We are finely dressed and have magnificent jewels, but we are tied to Mrs Waverley. I feel like a Chinese prostitute!'

'Whatever do you know about Chinese prostitutes?' asked Fanny, trying not to laugh.

'I read a most interesting book,' said Frederica.

'But now that we have agreed not to steal any more money, I don't see how I can buy any more books.'

She began to cry in earnest while the other two, new to demonstrations of affection, awkwardly patted her on the back.

Fanny was never to know how near Mrs Waverley came to canceling that drive. But Mrs Waverley had just made up her mind to tell Fanny to stay in her room while she got rid of the earl, when Lady Artemis arrived on the doorstep with six young misses, all demanding a training in the 'masculine arts' – by which they meant mathematics and science.

Flushed with success, Mrs Waverley, a born teacher, was soon setting up her 'schoolroom.' Fanny was forgotten.

Fanny had guessed that Mrs Waverley might change her mind and so she decided to be waiting in the hall when the earl arrived. She was wearing a new dress of soft white muslin, the high-waisted wrap-over bodice forming a V-neck, edged with a frill. Over it, she wore a pelisse of pale blue silk with a shawl collar and a wrap-over front, fastening under the bust with a belt. The long tight sleeves of the pelisse had frilled cuffs to match the frilled front edges and hem. On her head she wore a small swathed hat of white muslin decorated with pale blue feathers.

The earl arrived promptly at five o'clock. 'May I not make my bow to Mrs Waverley?' he asked as Fanny all but pushed him out of the door.

'She is too busy,' said Fanny quickly and indeed the babble of female voices coming from the drawing room upstairs underlined her remark.

Fanny felt suddenly shy of the earl. He looked very grand in a dark blue coat with brass buttons and deerskin breeches stretched without a wrinkle across his thighs. He was wearing top boots, a striped waistcoat, and a cravat that was a miracle of white muslin and starch. His curly brimmed beaver was set at just the right angle on his black hair.

Outside, he helped her into a phaeton and took his seat beside her and picked up the reins. There was no groom or tiger on the backstrap. The day was fine and sunny. Fanny suddenly felt free and young and happy and decided to forget about her troubles and enjoy every minute of her drive.

But when they got to the Park, she was introduced to one person after the other until her head reeled. Speculative eyes studied her gown, hard society eyes looked from her to the earl. Fanny remembered her undistinguished background and felt like an imposter. She grew silent and withdrawn and began to wish the ordeal would come to an end.

She heaved a little sigh of relief as they moved away from the ring. But the earl drove across Hyde Park, far away from the fashionables, and then reined in his horses and turned and smiled down at her. 'I am sorry about all the fuss,' he said. 'You are still a celebrity.'

'Can we go home now?' asked Fanny in a small voice.

'Most certainly. But will you not tell me what is troubling you?'

'I am not used to being the focus of attention,' said Fanny in a low voice.

'No, your beauty has been kept well hidden,' he agreed. 'There is something else, is there not? Trust in me, Miss Fanny. I would help you if I could.'

Fanny looked up at him nervously, but there was nothing but kindness and interest in his green eyes.

'I should not have come driving with you,' said Fanny, twisting her handkerchief in her gloved hands. 'You see, it will lead to vulgar speculation. I am an orphan. I do not know who my parents were. Society will think you are setting me up as your mistress.'

'Society does not know your background unless you have told them,' he pointed out. 'They believe you to be the eldest daughter of the rich Mrs Waverley.'

'But you know that not to be the case, and yet you took me driving. Why?'

'As I said before, Miss Fanny, you are very beautiful.'

'But not marriageable.'

His voice held a mocking note of laughter as he said, 'Dear me. Are you by any chance proposing to me?'

Fanny had a longing to embarrass him, to throw him, to make him feel as uncomfortable as she was feeling herself.

'Very well,' she said. 'Yes. Will you marry me, my Lord Tredair?'

He looked down into her sad blue eyes, at the

110

heaving of her delectable bosom, at the hint of long slim legs under the filmy gown. He thought of her courage in the balloon, he thought of lying on top of her in the balloon. He suddenly felt silly and light-hearted and very young.

'Why, yes, Miss Fanny, I will,' he said.

'Oh, I should have known you would mock me and laugh at me,' said Fanny bitterly. 'I was only jesting.'

'Alas. I was not,' he said. 'It seems like a good idea. You, me, marriage, I mean.'

'Sir, your parents, your lawyers, society would be appalled.'

'I do not rely on my parents for either money or permission. Will you marry me, Miss Fanny?'

'Why?'

'You excite me.'

'Not enough,' said Fanny, shaking her head sadly. 'There must be more than that. My looks will fade and lust will die and then you will tire of me.'

'That's a risk you and I will have to take. Have you not thought that *you* could just as easily tire of me? Society is full of jaded matrons. It is a wonder they do not put the Fashionable Impure out of business.'

'But I am not fickle.'

'That I have to take on trust. As my countess, you would have great freedom.'

'I had not thought of an aristocratic marriage,' said Fanny. 'In truth, I have not thought much of marriage at all. But aristocratic marriages have little to do with love and affection.'

'True. But there is always the exception.'

111

'I would never see you except to produce children. Gentlemen spend all the time in their clubs when they are not on the hunting field.'

The earl sat in silence, turning over what she had said. He certainly had planned to marry, but he had envisaged a marriage that would not interfere with his life. He certainly did not intend to stay in London. He meant to live quietly in the country and improve his estates. Might that not be taking her from one sort of prison to another?

'I do not racket about London all the time, Miss Fanny,' he said. 'I have a home in Bedfordshire called Denby Court. It is a pleasant country house with large acres. You might find me a dull stick. Have you ever lived in the country?'

Fanny shook her head.

'There are local balls and parties, but you might find it boring. Think on it. As my wife, you would have an entrée to society and money of your own and freedom. You might resent having to live in the country, away from all the fun.'

'If you loved me,' said Fanny, giving her handkerchief another wrench, 'it would not matter where we lived.'

He sighed. 'You are very young, and I fear you have been reading too many romances. Also, is there any question of you ever loving *me*?'

Fanny looked at him, wide-eyed, at his strong face, at those lazy, mocking green eyes, at that strong body, and then at his clever sensual mouth. She thought there was every possibility she could not only love him, but she might be well on the way to becoming obsessed by him, and that obsession could bring nothing but pain and hurt.

She blushed and said nothing.

Her body felt awkward and heavy, and her head throbbed.

'Perhaps we are going too fast,' she heard his voice say. 'Which orphanage did you attend?'

'Pevensey.'

'But that is an orphanage for young ladies. Surely someone must have paid to keep you there.'

'Mrs Waverley said we were all charity cases, that the orphanage occasionally took a few out of the kindness of their hearts.'

'Now that I find hard to believe.'

'Oh, how I would like to go there again,' cried Fanny, 'and ask them for myself.'

'Mrs Waverley would not give her permission?'

'Certainly not.'

'Then I shall go on your behalf, Miss Fanny.'

'Thank you. But I should like to see for myself. Do you understand?'

'I understand. But how are you to go about it?'

Fanny shook her head. 'I do not know.'

'Look,' he said urgently. 'You escape from time to time, do you not? Through the garden of Mr Fordyce's house? Could you not escape tomorrow morning early? I shall be waiting for you in the square.'

'I am fearful of discovery,' said Fanny. 'You see, we have been very lucky so far. The servants have not once seen us. But if we were caught, we could simply

113

say that we felt like a walk. But to be seen leaving with you . . . !'

'I think you will find the servants have noticed your escapades. Do not look so surprised. You cannot hide anything from servants.'

'But they would tell Mrs Waverley. If we try to leave by the front door, they bar our way.'

'Because that is what they had been told to do and would get into trouble should Mrs Waverley find you had left by the front door. But I think they turn a blind eye to your escapes by the garden. If you do not believe me, take that dragon, Mrs Ricketts, into your confidence. Here is a guinea. Give it to her from me and promise her more if she aids you.'

'If she tells on me, I shall be cast off.'

'I do not think so. Be cautious. Sound her out first. I shall wait for you at ten o'clock outside St George's Church.'

'Yes! Yes, I'll do it,' said Fanny.

'Then stop torturing that poor handkerchief.' He took it from her and held it up. It was a wisp of cambric. There was a light breeze blowing, and the handkerchief fluttered from his fingers and sailed into a stand of trees.

'I will get it for you,' he said climbing down. He walked into the stand of trees and then called urgently. 'Miss Fanny! Come here quickly.'

Fanny climbed down. The horses, startled, raised their heads and looked round and then began to crop the grass at their feet again.

Fanny went in among the trees. He was standing,

looking at the ground. 'What is it?' she cried, coming up to stand beside him.

He removed his hat and stood looking down at her. He held out the handkerchief. 'I am going to kiss you, Miss Fanny.'

'No!' said Fanny, backing away.

He smiled at her. 'It is the right of a man to try to kiss a pretty woman. Is it not the equal right of a pretty woman to want to kiss a man? Fie, for shame, Miss Fanny. You are a coward.'

'Not I,' said Fanny. 'I just don't want to kiss you.'

'Liar,' he mocked softly. 'You are not dying with love, but you are curious. Come here and kiss me.'

'No.'

'A fine bluestocking you make. Must I make your mind up for you?' He suddenly pulled her close, holding her tightly against his body. She could feel the beating of his heart.

Her body was melting, boneless, liquid fire. She looked up at him in a dazed way, her eyes dark, dark blue. He gave a stifled little exclamation and bent his mouth and kissed her. It was a chaste enough kiss as firm closed masculine lips met soft closed female ones. But neither was prepared for the blinding rush of black passion which that touch of lips caused. Neither was prepared for that maelstrom of feeling where they seemed to be whirling together deeper and deeper down into undiscovered depths.

The sound of a carriage passing nearby made them break apart.

Fanny could feel swollen nipples thrusting out

115

against the thin material of her gown and crossed her arms tightly over her breasts and shivered. 'Take me home,' she pleaded.

'Certainly,' he agreed, as formally as if nothing had taken place between them. He suddenly wanted to be alone with his thoughts. That simple kiss had shaken him as no other kiss had done. He distrusted the power she had over him. He had seen poor fellows the slave to some female's every whim and had sworn it would never happen to him. Fanny no longer seemed like a pretty and desirable girl, but a witch, an enchantress, and she spelled danger in every movement of her body. The breeze blew the fine material of her gown against her body and he looked away.

He wanted to tell her he would not see her on the morrow and then the thought of not seeing her caused him such a stab of pain that he said nothing.

He helped her down from the carriage and waited until she had disappeared inside the house before driving off.

Fanny went up to her room on shaking legs. She felt her innocence had been snatched from her in the Park. She felt she no longer owned her own soul. She kicked off her shoes and tore off her bonnet and lay face down on the bed, trying to fight the surgings and yearnings inside her body.

The door opened and Frederica and Felicity came in. Fanny sat up. 'What's the matter?' she demanded harshly.

'Nothing,' said Frederica with a shrug. 'Don't you look hot and cross! How was your drive?'

'Very interesting,' said Fanny, rallying with an effort. She told them all about the people she had met in the Park and described the clothes and carriages.

Then she said awkwardly, 'I want you to help me. Lord Tredair has offered to drive me to the orphanage tomorrow morning so that I might find out more about our backgrounds.'

There was a little silence and then Frederica asked, 'Why should he do that?'

'Because I told him I wanted to go,' snapped Fanny.

'We'll cover up for you,' said Felicity slowly, 'but don't betray us, Fanny, by running off with this lord.'

'I have no intention of running off with him, but if I did, what's it to you?'

'We are none of us marriageable,' said Frederica. 'For all we now distrust Mrs Waverley, we must always be grateful to her. I agree with her principles. If you become Tredair's mistress, I will never see or speak to you again.'

'What if I became his wife?' demanded Fanny.

'Don't be silly. An earl? Marry *you*!'

'I have no interest in any man,' sighed Fanny, sinking back against her pillows and staring at the ceiling.

'See that it stays that way,' said Frederica coldly. 'We can manipulate Mrs Waverley, now that we know how her mind works, into giving us a more pleasant and freer life. Don't spoil it. Promise!'

'I won't spoil anything,' sighed Fanny, feeling she was becoming a practiced liar. Had she not already promised Mrs Waverley not to encourage the earl in any way? What on earth would Mrs Waverley, let alone these sisters of hers, think if they knew she had asked the earl to marry her?

After they had left, Fanny wondered whether to send for Mrs Ricketts and bribe her as the earl had suggested. But she found she had not the courage. If it did not work, then she would not be able to go to the orphanage on the morrow.

SEVEN

'There she goes again . . . and at this time of the morning!' said Mrs Ricketts to the cook, Mrs Smiles.

'Which one of them is it?' asked the cook.

'Just caught a glimpse out the back,' said Mrs Ricketts. 'Miss Fanny, I think.'

'Mistress would be in a right taking if she knew they were getting loose,' pointed out the cook, not for the first time. 'Good thing she's not giving lessons this morning.'

'They never stay away long,' said Mrs Ricketts. ''T ain't natteral, keeping 'em in the house from morning till night. Anyway, we're told to see none of them go out the front door, so there's no cause to interfere. There's one thing about this odd household that suits me – no men. No butler puffing and blowing and giving orders and not doing any work hisself. But we're past marriage, Mrs Smiles, so it's comfortable for us. But young things like that should be out at parties and have plenty of beaux.' In the cases of both the housekeeper and the cook, the Mrs was a courtesy title.

'Madam doesn't know what you think, I hope,' said Mrs Smiles.

'No. She doesn't think that servants think at all. She's really like the rest of the quality. She preaches on about equality, but that don't apply to the servants hall. Miss Fanny'll be back soon enough.'

'But it's different now,' pointed out the cook, brushing flour from her nose with the back of her hand. 'Mr Fordyce is in that house next door.'

'Not yet,' said Mrs Ricketts. 'He moves in next week with a staff of servants. Reckon I'll need to have a word with the girls then.'

Fanny flew across the square, expecting any moment to hear an angry voice calling her back. She let out a little gasp of dismay as she reached the pillared entrance of St George's Church, for there was no sign of the earl. The morning was chilly, and she wrapped her old woollen cloak more tightly about her. She felt very conspicuous standing alone on the steps.

She heard a carriage approaching and moved behind one of the pillars. It came to a stop and she peered around.

The earl! Thank goodness.

'I thought you were not going to come,' she said breathlessly as she climbed into the open carriage beside him.

'I always keep my word, Miss Fanny,' he said. 'Off we go to find your past!'

He drove along in silence. Fanny was wearing her coal scuttle bonnet and looked every inch an orphanage girl, he reflected. He broke the silence at last.

'Do not pin your hopes on this visit,' he said. 'Do not cherish any dreams that your parents are noble. It will probably turn out to be as you have heard.'

'All I have heard is that I was a foundling,' said Fanny. 'A foundling, and no one knows who my parents are or were. But I cannot believe it.'

'What name were you given at the orphanage?'

'Miss Bride – after the church where I was found.'

'And the two other girls?'

'Bride as well.'

'Do you mean you were all abandoned on the same church doorstep?'

'Hardly,' laughed Fanny. 'We arrived at the orphanage at the same time. They said they were tired of inventing names and so they called us all the same.'

'And so the other two are foundlings as well?'

'I do not know. I seem to be the only one who was given at least one crumb of information.'

The streets and houses flew past as his horses were urged to quicken their pace. Fanny began to feel cold with worry as the orphanage approached. She wished now she had put on something grand, not her 'walking' outfit that made her look like a charity girl, that made her look as if she had never left the place. She comforted herself in the earl's title and elegance.

He drove through the curved stone arch of the

courtyard and reined in his horse under the familiar brass oil lamp over the door.

As he was tethering the reins to a post in the yard, the great door of the orphanage opened and Fanny recognized Mr Wilks, the chairman.

He did not recognize her, though his glance only flicked over her and came to rest inquiringly on the earl.

'We were not warned of any visit,' said Mr Wilks in his querulous, high, fluting voice.

He was a thin, spare Scotsman who affected a sort of genteel dandyism, his bottle green waistcoat being hung with a great many seals and fobs and his new hessian boots dangling with little gold tassels. He had pale blue-gray wary eyes and long bony hands with prominent knuckles.

The earl approached him and made a bow. 'I am Tredair,' said the earl, 'and this is one of your former charges, Miss Fanny Bride.'

Mr Wilks looked startled, and Fanny was sure she saw a gleam of fear darting across his pale eyes.

'What is the meaning of this visit, my lord?' demanded Mr Wilks, his voice shrill. 'Our humble orphanage is pleased that the great Earl of Tredair should visit us, but it is most inconvenient – *most* inconvenient,' he added, looking over one hunched shoulder as if seeking help.

'We will not take up much of your time,' said the earl pleasantly. 'Miss Waverley, as she now is, is naturally anxious to discover the identity of her parents.'

'Step inside, my lord,' said Mr Wilks. 'This is too painful a subject to be discussed outside.'

He stood aside to let them pass. As Fanny came abreast of him, Mr Wilks muttered, 'How could you, you ungrateful girl? Did we not do our best for you?'

Fanny opened her mouth to reply, but he strode ahead of her shouting, 'Mrs Goern!'

The door to the orphanage office opened and Mrs Goern stood there, looking the same as Fanny had remembered her, fat and florid, like an overstuffed, heavily embroidered cushion.

'May I present the Earl of Tredair,' gabbled Mr Wilks, 'and Miss Fanny. You remember our Fanny.'

'Oh, yes,' said Mrs Goern slowly. 'What is the problem?'

'Perhaps if we could all sit down . . . ?' said the earl, moving into the stuffy office.

Mr Wilks sat behind a desk with Mrs Goern beside him. Fanny and the earl sat facing them.

'Miss Fanny has come to find out her background,' said Mr Wilks.

'That was a great mistake,' said Mrs Goern severely. 'You are a very lucky girl to have been adopted by a great lady like Mrs Waverley. Is this how you reward her?'

'Save us your strictures, madam,' said the earl coldly. 'Simply tell Miss Waverley what she wants to know.'

Mrs Goern's fat lips disappeared into a thin line. 'If you will excuse me, my lord,' she said, getting to her feet, 'I will fetch the books.'

The earl noticed that Mr Wilks looked at the director with a certain amount of alarm, and that Mrs Goern gave him a little reassuring nod.

They waited in silence. The earl rose and went to the barred window and looked out into the courtyard. There he saw Mrs Goern giving instructions to a surly-looking individual. The man touched his cap and sauntered off in the direction of the stables.

After what seemed a very long time, Mrs Goern returned, bearing two large ledgers.

'You will find, my lord,' she said, 'that Miss Fanny came to us from the Foundling Hospital.'

'In the City?'

'No, my lord. In Greenwich.'

'Pray tell me why a baby found on the steps of St Bride's in Fleet Street should be sent all the way to Greenwich?'

'If Miss Fanny knew that much, my lord, then it was a waste of your time to bring you here,' said Mrs Goern. 'I do not know why she was sent to Greenwich, but that is the case.'

'Then tell me, Mrs Goern, why it is that this orphanage, which houses young ladies with relatives rich enough to place them here, should accept charity cases?'

'Through the kindness of our hearts, my lord,' said Mr Wilks piously.

Fanny sat with her head bowed, her hopes in ruins. She had never really believed that story about her being a foundling. Now she felt like a romantic fool.

The earl felt himself becoming very angry indeed.

'You will forgive me if I point out that there is nothing in your bearing and manner that leads me to suppose either of you know the meaning of kindness or charity,' he said.

'Ho!' bristled Mrs Goern. 'And just what is your business with Miss Fanny?'

'Miss Waverley is a friend of mine,' said the earl. He smiled down at Fanny. But Fanny did not see that smile, she only heard the words. If only he had said, 'The lady I hope to marry.' But, of course, he could never marry her now.

'I realize this is a shock to you,' said Mr Wilks in a wheedling tone. 'And I forgive you. Pray take some refreshment.'

'No,' said the earl haughtily. 'Not with such as you. Since you are not prepared to be of further assistance, we may as well leave. I assume you will tell me that the other two girls are also foundlings from Greenwich?'

'But yes, my lord,' exclaimed Mr Wilks. 'So kind of Mrs Waverley to relieve us of three of our charity cases.'

The earl glanced out of the window where a long crocodile of girls was now walking round the yard. He studied them for a moment and then said thoughtfully, 'How odd that the three should perhaps be the most beautiful and intelligent girls in the orphanage?'

'We have many such,' said Mrs Goern with a tight expression. 'Believe me, my lord, this interview is as distasteful to us as it is to you.'

'I doubt it,' said the earl. 'Come, Miss Fanny.'

Too broken in spirit to ask any questions herself, Fanny followed him out. She was aware of the envious looks of the girls as she climbed into the earl's smart carriage. She could not even bear to search their faces to see if there was anyone left in the orphanage she still knew.

The earl drove off in silence and after they had gone a little way, slowed his team to an amble. 'I do not know why they should lie, Miss Fanny,' he said, 'but I am sure they are lying. I think a visit to that foundling hospital in Greenwich is called for.'

'No,' said Fanny with a shudder. 'No more. Enough. I have been living on dreams.'

'As you will. But I would be happy to go there for you.'

Fanny shook her head and a tear rolled down onto her glove.

'Please do not cry,' said the earl. 'It does not matter. Would you like to marry me?'

'I cannot . . . now,' said Fanny. 'In time, you would regret having allied yourself to someone of no background whatsoever.'

'That is for me to decide, dear girl.'

'Have you considered what society would say? Your family? Your friends?'

'They would say a great deal if they knew. But they won't. As far as they are concerned you are Mrs Waverley's daughter.'

'Mrs Waverley will never let me marry.'

'If she has a fondness for you . . . if she has one

spark of affection in her whole body . . . she will let you marry.'

'Don't speak of it,' said Fanny. 'You do not know her. It is not possible.'

He tried to protest, but Fanny looked so white and ill that he fell silent.

He dropped her outside the church, promising to call, but Fanny barely heard him. All she wanted to do was to get safely home and bury her head in her pillow and have a good cry.

The earl drove off thoughtfully. There was a mystery there. Did the mystery lie in that whisper of Clorinda he had heard from the Prince Regent? Were the girls all royal bastards? If that was the case, then both foundling hospital and orphanage would know it was more than their lives were worth to speak the truth. But if Mrs Waverley could be persuaded to keep quiet about Fanny's birth and to give him permission to marry the girl, then there would be no fuss and no scandal.

By the time he reached his own home, he was feeling much more cheerful. It was as well he did not know what was happening in Hanover Square.

Fanny had climbed in the library window and had darted up the stairs to her room. She swung open the door and let out a gasp as she saw Mrs Waverley sitting in a chair by the window.

'Come in, you scheming, lying, ungrateful girl,' said Mrs Waverley wrathfully. Fanny entered the room slowly, pulling off her bonnet. She stood facing Mrs Waverley.

'I have reason to believe you went to the orphanage with Lord Tredair,' said Mrs Waverley. 'I told you, you were a foundling. But my name and protection is not enough for you. How dare you make a spectacle of yourself by driving through the streets unchaperoned with a *man*?'

'I had to find out,' said Fanny warily. 'He wants to marry me.'

'You must be mistaken,' said Mrs Waverley. 'Men like Tredair do not marry girls like you.'

'Lord Tredair says that as far as the world is concerned, I am your daughter, and therefore there can be no reason to stop the marriage,' said Fanny. 'How did you know I had been to the orphanage?'

'Poor Mrs Goern sent me a message. She was most distressed. There is no question of you marrying Lord Tredair or anyone, Fanny. If you do not behave yourself, I shall turn you out. Yes! Turn you out into the street, you ungrateful girl. Have I not given you the best of everything? Have I not taught you my principles? Men are filthy beasts . . . beasts. How can you do this to me . . . me . . . who has loved you like a mother?'

Fat tears rolled down Mrs Waverley's face and plopped in the silk of her lap.

Fanny knelt on the floor beside her. 'Don't cry,' she whispered. 'I shall forget him. Please don't cry. I am not ungrateful.'

Mrs Waverley slowly caressed Fanny's blond hair.

'Then we will say no more about it,' she said softly. 'I would not turn you out, Fanny. I said that in anger. I love you dearly. I am sorry about your background

– a foundling and a bastard. But such things are not a disadvantage if you stay unmarried. Promise me you will never see Lord Tredair again.'

'I promise,' said Fanny, too crushed to realize she would soon regret that promise.

'Then kiss me, my child, and we will say no more about it.'

Fanny rose and gently kissed Mrs Waverley's wet cheek.

Mrs Waverley rose as well, took out a handkerchief, and dried her eyes. She peered at the watch pinned to her bosom. 'Good gracious. Lady Artemis will be here at any moment,' she cried.

Fanny was relieved to see her go.

She kicked off her shoes and flung herself face down on the bed.

But she was not to be allowed any peace.

Mrs Waverley had only been gone a few moments when the door opened and Frederica and Felicity came in.

'Go away,' groaned Fanny. 'I can't bear any more.'

'No, we will not go away,' said Frederica. 'Your escapade was discovered, and the servants have been threatened with dismissal should one of us be found outside the house again. You fool, Fanny. I bet you found out that we are all bastards and foundlings.'

'Yes,' said Fanny dismally. 'But Tredair is sure they are lying.'

'Tredair, Tredair,' mocked Felicity. 'What is it to him?'

'He wants to marry me,' said Fanny, sitting up.

'Rubbish,' said Frederica. 'We don't marry. You know that. He wants you as his mistress.'

'No,' said Fanny wildly.

'Oh, yes. Do you think he will come near you after today?'

'Yes,' said Fanny mutinously.

'Well, he won't,' said Frederica. 'You'll see. I will never, I swear, get myself in such a state over any man. Mrs Waverley is right. Look how unhappy you are. And look at the mess you have landed us in, you wicked thing! Now we can't get out anywhere because of your mawkish desire to marry a lord! Now we know that we are as bad as you, foundlings and bastards.'

'Shut up,' said Fanny. 'Foundlings we may be, but where is the proof that we are bastards?'

'We're trash, trash, trash,' mocked Frederica.

'Leave me alone,' screamed Fanny, picking up the water jug from beside the bed, 'or I will throw this at your heads!'

'We have no intention of leaving until you come to your senses,' said Felicity. Then both girls ducked as Fanny leapt to her feet, seized the water jug, and sent it flying. Frederica and Felicity scampered out of the room, just as Fanny followed up the water jug with a bottle of perfume that smashed against the closing door. The whole room reeked of Young Miss in Her Youth. Fanny began to cry again.

Question time in the drawing room. Miss Follity-Benson was the only lady who was not enjoying herself. She could not get her sums to add up. She

130

was not experiencing any of the joys of education promised her and felt obscurely resentful of the domineering Mrs Waverley.

On impulse she raised her hand.

'Yes, Miss Follity-Benson?' cooed Mrs Waverley.

'Would you not say that since women are made to bear children, it is going against nature if they do not do so?' asked Miss Follity-Benson.

'Not exactly,' said Mrs Waverley with a frown. 'London is full of unwanted children as is the rest of the British Isles. Any woman deciding not to have children is doing society a service.'

'But you have three daughters,' pointed out Miss Follity-Benson.

Mrs Waverley suddenly saw a way of spiking the Earl of Tredair's guns.

'Alas,' she said. 'They are not my daughters. I do what I can to help the unwanted and unloved, you know. My three girls are foundlings and bastards and can never marry. I adopted them.'

There were exclamations of shock and surprise. Lady Artemis found she was sitting with her mouth wide open and shut it. What marvelous, wonderful news! Tredair was safe from Miss Fanny.

But Miss Follity-Benson had a kind heart. 'I am sure I speak for all, Mrs Waverley,' she said, 'when I assure you that not one of us here will breathe a word of this.'

Lady Artemis thought there was a certain look of disappointment on Mrs Waverley's face and wondered why.

'You are most kind,' said Mrs Waverley briskly. 'Now, next question . . . ?'

Breakfasts were those affairs held at three o'clock in the afternoon. The one Lord Tredair attended with Mr Fordyce the next day was in the grounds of a large house in Kensington. The weather had turned warm and sunny, and he was strolling about with Mr Fordyce admiring the gardens when he noticed the arrival of Lady Artemis. He felt more charitably disposed toward her than he had done before because she had helped to clean that nasty kitchen with such good will.

He noticed with amusement that Lady Artemis seemed to have a prime piece of gossip. For she moved busily from group to group, whispering and chattering, and then he heard oohs and aahs of surprise.

Mr Fordyce noticed the busily gossiping Lady Artemis as well. 'I wonder what she is talking about,' he said.

'No doubt we will hear soon enough,' said the earl. 'I do not think I shall stay for the breakfast. I came to see the gardens, you know. I shall be like Brummell, who advocates one should stay just long enough to make one's presence known, and then leave.'

'I cannot protest at your going,' laughed Mr Fordyce, 'for that leaves the field open to me.'

'With Lady Artemis?'

'Exactly, my friend.'

The earl smiled and began to move away. As he reached the entrance to the gardens, his host, Mr

Tommy Blythe, bore down on him. 'Leaving so soon, Tredair?'

'Alas, yes. I have a pressing appointment.'

'You always have pressing appointments,' grumbled Mr Blythe. 'Why do you come to the Season if not to stay at the functions?'

'Perhaps I am looking for wife.'

'Never! A hardened bachelor like you? Talking of marriage, that pretty creature you went ballooning with is the talk of the party.'

'Miss Fanny was very brave,' said the earl. 'Quite a heroine.'

'Yes, but such shocking news. I could hardly believe my ears. To think I sent cards to the Waverleys! But as m'wife pointed out, Mrs Waverley at least knows what's what and refused to attend, or we would have to have sent them packing.'

'What are you gabbling on about?' demanded the earl crossly.

'Why, Lady Artemis was at Mrs Waverley's yesterday, and she ups and tells Lady Artemis and a parcel of society misses that her three girls are adopted and not only that, but that they are bastards and foundlings!'

The earl's hands clenched into fists. 'What a hateful, scheming, cruel women,' he raged.

Mr Blythe took a step back. 'Oh, I don't know,' he said. 'She's done a great thing. She could easily have fooled society and foisted her girls onto some of us, don't you think?'

But the earl was already walking away.

He drove the mile from Kensington to Hanover Square where he demanded an audience with Mrs Waverley. He was shown up to the drawing room. The blinds were drawn and Mrs Waverley was lying on a chaise longue by the window.

'Forgive me for not rising, my lord,' she said. 'I have had an exhausting day.'

'Very exhausting, madam,' he said coldly. 'Ruining the reputation of your adopted daughters must have been quite tiring.'

'I did it for the best,' said Mrs Waverley. 'This letter will explain why. It is from Fanny.'

The earl silently took the letter and read it. Then he went across and jerked up one of the blinds and stood by the window and read it again.

'Lord Tredair,' he read, 'I will always be grateful to you for taking me to the orphanage. But I fear I may have misled you as to my feelings toward you. I shall never marry, and it would be best if I never see you again. Your humble and obedient servant, Fanny Waverley.'

'You forced her to write this,' he said angrily.

'Not I,' said Mrs Waverley mournfully. 'My lord, Fanny is a headstrong girl. Can you see me forcing her to do anything?'

'Yes,' he said. 'You could threaten to throw her out.'

'I would never do that,' said Mrs Waverley. 'You see, I love Fanny.'

'I doubt if you love anyone other than yourself,' he said bitterly. 'Good day to you, ma'am.'

He let the letter flutter to the floor and strode from the room.

Mrs Waverley leaned back, feeling almost as exhausted as she had claimed to be. It had taken quite a bit of effort to forge that letter. She had expected him to call and had told the servants that at the first sight of him, the young ladies were to be sent to their rooms and kept there, and the name of the visitor was not to be divulged. Mrs Waverley rose and retrieved the letter, held it over the fireplace and set light to a corner of it with a brimstone match, and waited until the whole letter was alight before dropping it into the hearth.

The end of Lord Tredair. The end of a nasty upsetting chapter. But she had done it for the best. Fanny was safe and would never leave her now.

The house in Hanover Square settled back into its previous gloom. Mrs Waverley gave no more lessons, nor did she take the girls out walking around the square.

Mr Fordyce moved in next door, but when he called on Mrs Waverley, he was refused admittance.

Across the square Lady Artemis was suffering from a new feeling, that of an acute guilty conscience. Lord Tredair now went out of his way to avoid her. Mr Fordyce had told her that he was shocked she had gossiped about the Waverley girls' dreadful backgrounds, and she appeared to have lost even his admiration. She called at the Waverleys' and sent flowers and gifts, but she was turned away and the gifts and flowers were returned. The house crouched in silence and no one but tradesmen came or went.

The friendship of the three girls was under a strain. Felicity and Frederica could not help blaming Fanny for their new incarceration. The long days dragged after each other, the sun shone, and merry voices sounded from the square outside to underline their boredom and isolation within.

And then, just when they thought they could not bear it any longer, a new worry descended on them.

Mrs Waverley was missing her classes. She had decided to send a note to Lady Artemis asking her to resume her attendance. She enjoyed teaching and she enjoyed showing off the richness of her mansion and jewels to these society ladies.

She planned to recommence as soon as possible. She would wear her new purple silk gown and perhaps a very expensive brooch. Something simple, but rich enough to make their eyes pop. There was that diamond brooch of Fanny's. That would look very well against her purple silk.

At first when Ricketts told her the brooch was missing from Miss Fanny's box, she was not very worried, merely commanding the housekeeper to search the other girls' rooms. But when it transpired the brooch was really missing, Mrs Waverley became angry and summoned the girls and the whole household. If that brooch was not put back on her dressing table by noon the next day, she said wrathfully, then she would call in the Runners.

The girls retreated to Fanny's room for a council of war.

'What are we to do?' asked Felicity, white-lipped. 'Any Runner worth his salt will call at the nearest pawn shops and we will be undone. No one is going to believe in the nonexistent Lady Tremblant. We cannot take any jewelry to get it back, for she now has had all our jewel boxes locked in her room. What are we to do?'

'It is all my fault,' said Fanny. She thought of the guinea Lord Tredair had given her to bribe Ricketts. But it would not go far in getting the brooch redeemed. Tredair! *He* would know what to do. If only she could see him. Why couldn't she see him! She knew he lived in St James's Square, for she had read a description of a rout at his town house some time ago.

She dared not tell the girls, for they would cry out against it. She had given her solemn promise to Mrs Waverley not to see Lord Tredair again. But surely God would not concern Himself with the broken promises of a bastard and foundling.

'Leave me,' she said. 'I will get it back.'

'How?' demanded the other two.

'It is better you do not know,' said Fanny, and refused to be drawn.

EIGHT

Fanny waited until later that evening and then slipped quietly down the stairs to the housekeeper's parlor.

'Well, Miss Fanny?' said Mrs Ricketts, looking up from a piece of sewing, 'What can I do for you?'

Fanny summoned up her courage. Mrs Ricketts was using her genteel company voice that was somehow more daunting than as if she had spoken in her normal country accents.

'I have to go out tonight,' she blurted out.

Mrs Ricketts put down her sewing. 'Come in, Miss Fanny, and close the door behind you.' She waited until Fanny was seated and then said, 'I know you've been slipping out before, out the garden at the back.'

'Oh, Mrs Ricketts . . .'

'I didn't worry overmuch,' said Mrs Ricketts, reaching to a bottle on a side table and pouring herself a measure of gin. 'You always came back quick enough and I reckoned it didn't do no harm to anyone.' Her country accent became stronger as she went on, 'But you got us all in mortal trouble the day you went off with that Lord Tredair.'

'I went to the orphanage,' said Fanny. 'I had to try to find out about my parents.'

'And all you found out was bad news,' said Mrs Ricketts sympathetically. She tossed back her glass of gin and put the glass down on the table with a decisive little click. 'Trouble is, the whole of London must know that news by now.'

'What do you mean?'

'Mrs Waverley was preaching or whatever she does to that party of ladies brought here by Lady Artemis. I was bringing in the refreshments just as a snippity little chit asked her about women's natural duty to bear children or something. Mrs Waverley ups and says how there's too many unwanted brats around and that she took you three from the orphanage and that you're bastards and foundlings. I reckon you're all foundlings all right, but no call to leap to the conclusion that all your parents never bothered to get married.'

Fanny raised her hands to her hot cheeks. 'Why should she ruin us in the eyes of society?'

'Keep you at home,' said Mrs Ricketts. 'See, that way no one'll want to marry you.'

'So that is why Lord Tredair never came back,' said Fanny in a choked voice.

'Oh, he come back all right, and we had instructions to put you girls in your rooms and see you didn't come out. I don't know what madam said, but my lord left here in a fine taking.'

Fanny sat with her head bowed. The fact that she was about to attempt to see Lord Tredair again after having given her solemn promise not to do so had weighed heavily on her conscience. Now, she did not care. Would not any prisoner in Newgate lie and lie again if he knew it was the means to escape?

'Now, why do you want to go out this night?' asked Mrs Ricketts.

'It's that diamond brooch,' said Fanny. 'I have to get it back.'

'From the pawnshop,' said Mrs Ricketts, nodding her head.

'How did you know . . . ?'

'Betty, the housemaid, was in Oxford Street one day and saw Miss Felicity going into the pawnbrokers. She followed her when she come out, thinking if it was bad mischief she had better report it to me. Well, she then followed Miss Felicity to Hatchard's where young miss bought a book and then followed her home. She told me. We talked about it. You're all laden down with jewels like heathen princesses, so we reckoned that you was pawning the things for pin money. I checked the jewel boxes when you were out walking and there was only little bits and pieces missing. When she asked me to take that inventory, I was sore troubled, for I knew I would have to speak up so as not to let the blame fall on any of the servants. Then the jewels were all there and I wondered how you had done it. Later, I checked again and found the diamond brooch missing, so I knew you'd taken that to redeem the others. Now, you are going to ask Lord Tredair for the money to get the brooch back.'

Fanny nodded her head, and then held out a guinea. 'That's from Lord Tredair, Mrs Ricketts. I should have given it to you before. Before I went to the orphanage, he told me to give it to you. He said I would find out you already knew. He said to tell you he would give you more if you continued to aid me.'

'What is his lordship's interest in you, Miss Fanny?' said Mrs Ricketts, taking the guinea and putting it in her apron pocket.

'He wishes to marry me.'

'Are you sure, Miss Fanny? A man like his lordship could get any woman he wanted.'

'I think he means it at the moment, but, of course, he would never really forget my background.'

She looked hopefully at the housekeeper as if waiting for a contradiction, but Mrs Ricketts nodded her head and said, 'That's the way of the world. Blood is all in all in them families. Look at Lord Ponsonby what married Miss Linklater, a merchant's daughter, for her money. All was lovey-dovey in the beginning, but now he jeers at her on every occasion and treats her something cruel.'

'How do you know this?' asked Fanny, momentarily diverted.

'Let me see, Lord Ponsonby's scullery maid told the page at Mr Brough's, him next door to Lady Artemis, and the page told her footman, who told the footman next door, not Mr Fordyce's side, but the other, Sir Jeffrey Banks, who told our Mary who told me. But to return to your problem, if you go out, you'll need to go out late. Mrs Waverley doesn't fall asleep till eleven o'clock, and I can't let you out on your own at that time.'

'*Please*, Mrs Ricketts.'

'Also, you can't go calling at a gentleman's town house. It would ruin your reputation.'

'I haven't got a reputation to ruin,' pointed out Fanny bitterly.

'They may call you a foundling and bastard, but if you're seen going into his town house, they'd call you whore as well.'

'What am I to do?' wailed Fanny.

The housekeeper sat buried in thought. Then she said slowly, 'I could get Betty to tell Mrs Waverley I was indisposed, just in case she sends for me. Then I could go to his lordship's house and tell him to come here, down to the servants hall.'

'But surely one of the servants will talk!' cried Fanny.

'Not if I don't,' said Mrs Ricketts grimly. 'Mrs Waverley gives me absolute control of the staff.'

Fanny brightened. 'But I have an idea! In that case, there is no need for me to meet him. I can just give you a letter . . .'

Her voice trailed off before the housekeeper's withering stare. 'Miss Fanny. You can't ask an earl to go to the pawn for you in a letter!' Mrs Ricketts got to her feet, took down a clean tumbler, poured a measure of gin into it, and then one into her own tumbler.

Then she took the small smoke-blackened kettle off the fire and added hot water to each glass.

Mrs Ricketts handed Fanny a glass and raised her own. 'No heeltaps,' she said.

'No heeltaps,' echoed Fanny, tossing off her own. She coughed and spluttered as the mixture of gin and hot water burned her throat. 'Why heeltaps?' she asked hoarsely. 'It's silly, but I've often wondered.'

'Well, you know what heeltaps are?'

'Yes,' said Fanny. 'They're that crescent shaped piece of metal on the heel of a boot to protect it from wear.'

'Practically all of the drinks used to be sweet and sticky,' said Mrs Ricketts. 'What was left at the bottom of the glass was a crescent of sticky liquid. No heeltaps means drain it to the last drop. Now, you'd best be off and leave me to find my lord!'

Mrs Ricketts waited until Fanny had gone and then put on her cloak and bonnet and left by way of the area steps after informing the other women servants that a gentleman would be using the servants hall for an interview with Miss Fanny, and they were not to breathe a word to anyone. They were to go to bed and not stir, no matter what they heard.

The night was chilly and a high wind had risen. The parish lamps flickered in their glass globes as she hurried across the square. She knew Lord Tredair's address. Mrs Ricketts knew the addresses of all the nobles in London. She read all the gossip columns and had a staggering memory.

She did not really have much hope of finding Lord

Tredair at home. It was Wednesday night and balls at Almack's were always held on Wednesdays.

She finally reached St James's Square and mounted the shallow steps to Lord Tredair's town house and hammered on the knocker. A butler looking as grand as an archbishop answered the door and told her in tones of haughty surprise that the earl was not at home.

Mrs Ricketts stood, baffled, not really wanting to give up so easily. She made her way to Almack's in King Street and stood on the corner. Even at her age and with her grim appearance and sensible dress she knew that any female standing on a corner at that time of night would be taken for a prostitute, so she made her way to Oxford Street until she found an orange seller. Taking out the guinea Fanny had given her, she purchased the whole basket of oranges and went back to Almack's and stood across the road, watching the long windows and the people coming and going in the entrance.

She was just about to give up because it suddenly seemed all so hopeless. If Lord Tredair was enjoying himself, if he was, after all, there, he might not emerge until five in the morning.

Then she saw the earl standing on the step, drawing on his gloves.

She hurried across the road. 'Oranges. Buy my oranges,' she called.

One of the flunkies rushed toward her. Hawkers on the steps of Almack's! There would be revolution next.

The earl had quickly masked his surprise at the sight of the Waverley housekeeper. He waved the flunky away. 'Leave the good woman alone,' he said.

He jerked his head slightly. Mrs Waverley fell back as he walked away and then followed him at a discreet distance. A man stopped her. 'How much are your oranges, grandma?' he said.

'Oh, go away!' yelled Mrs Ricketts, pushing past him.

The earl was waiting in the shadow of a porticoed entrance on the corner.

'Masquerade party?' he asked.

'My lord,' said Mrs Ricketts, 'you are to follow me. Miss Fanny wishes to speak to you.'

He raised his thin eyebrows in haughty surprise. 'I was given a letter by Miss Fanny in which she said she never wanted to see me again.'

'Miss Fanny handed it to you personal?' exclaimed Mrs Ricketts.

'No, Mrs Waverley.'

'Then she wrote it herself, Mrs Waverley, I mean,' said Mrs Ricketts.

'Are you sure?'

'Stands to reason, don't it, my lord?'

'Very well. Give me that basket and lead the way.'

'No, my lord. You will simply draw attention to yourself. I will go ahead and get Miss Fanny. You are to go down the area steps. You will find the door unlocked. Wait in the servants hall.'

She scurried off before he could reply.

He tried to tell himself he should not go. The

Waverleys, all of them, meant trouble. But the longing to see Fanny again was stronger than anything.

He made his way at a leisurely pace through the streets. The wind was even stronger than it had been earlier, roaring through the chimney tops and sending snakes of smoke from the spinning cowls down into the streets below. He was just turning into Hanover Square when a vis-à-vis drew alongside him and came to a stop. In it sat Lady Artemis and her maid. 'My lord!' she cried. 'Where are you bound?'

'On my own affairs,' he said stiffly.

'Why do you regard me so coldly?' cried Lady Artemis. 'Have I done something to offend you?'

'Yes, madam,' said the earl. 'You gossiped to beat the band about the Waverley girls, and now they are become a sad joke and will never escape from that prison in which they are incarcerated.'

'I only repeated what Mrs Waverley told me,' said Lady Artemis turning pink.

'You should have known that such a piece of news would have been better kept to yourself. Pray, drive on. The night air is cold.'

'But cannot I explain . . . ?'

'You are a malicious tattletale, madam. Pray drive on before I say something much worse.'

The vis-à-vis moved on.

The earl waited until he had seen Lady Artemis enter her own house and quickly made his way down the area steps of the Waverley mansion. As promised, the door was open. He went into the servants

146

hall, which was lit by one solitary tallow candle on the middle of the table.

After he had been waiting only a few moments, the door opened and Fanny came in. Her eyes looked black and enormous in the flickering candle-light.

'Pray be seated, my lord,' she said in a whisper. 'Did Mrs Ricketts tell you why I sent for you?'

He shook his head. He sat down and Fanny pulled out a chair next to him and sat down as well and clasped her hands on the table.

'Now you are here, my lord,' she said in a low voice, 'I find it much harder to explain things to you than I could possibly have imagined. Oh, why are you in evening dress!'

A flash of humor lit his green eyes. 'I have been at Almack's, Miss Fanny. They are sticklers for the rules. I could hardly attend in anything else.'

What Fanny really meant was that evening dress made him seem remote, less approachable. The candlelight flickered on the diamond pin in his cravat and on the little diamond chips in the buttons of his evening coat. He had placed his bicorne on the table and his hair gleamed with purple lights.

'I think you had better begin,' he prompted gently, 'or we shall be here all night.'

Fanny took a deep breath and then in an urgent whisper she told him about pawning the jewels, cul-minating in the pawning of the diamond brooch and the desperate need to get it back.

He leaned back easily in his chair as she spoke, one hand resting on the table, the other in his pocket. His face was an inscrutable mask.

The Earl of Tredair was deeply shocked.

He could forgive Fanny all sorts of dreadful backgrounds. Her birth was not her fault. But stealing! Surely that betrayed a low streak in the blood that would come out again and again.

Although he said nothing, Fanny could feel him moving away from her. It was as if a sudden frost had settled on the servants hall.

'And why should you think I would redeem the brooch for you?' he asked when she had finished.

'Because . . . I thought . . . I thought you cared for me a little,' said Fanny.

'I cared for you more than a little,' he said. 'But I cannot entertain any warm affections toward a thief. And you are a thief, Miss Fanny. Mrs Waverley is eccentric and confines you to the house. You are little better than prisoners. But what would your lot have been had she left you in the orphanage?'

Fanny hung her head.

'Exactly. With no relatives to claim you, you would at best have become a governess if you were lucky or a companion, but more likely some sort of genteel drudge. Did you write me a letter?'

'No,' said Fanny.

'Yes. I should have known. But it does not matter now. Where is this pawnbroker?'

'In Oxford Street. At the corner of North Audley.'

'And do you have the ticket?'

Fanny took a crumpled ticket out of the bodice of her gown and mutely held it out to him.

'I shall go first thing in the morning,' he said, 'and my servant will bring the brooch to Mrs Ricketts.'

'Thank you,' whispered Fanny, brokenly.

'Then if that is all, I shall take my leave.'

'You don't understand,' said Fanny urgently, taking hold of his sleeve. 'You must understand . . .'

He firmly disengaged the clutching little hand from his sleeve and stood up. Fanny shivered as she looked up into his cold green eyes, as cold as the Atlantic.

'Good-bye, Miss Fanny,' he said. 'We shall not meet again.'

She remained seated, her head bowed. The door closed quietly, and then she could hear him mounting the area steps.

'I heard him go,' said Mrs Ricketts, coming into the servants hall. 'Going to do it, is he?'

'Yes, Mrs Ricketts. But he has now a bottomless disgust of me. He called me a thief.' Fanny burst into tears.

'Shhh. Quietly now,' said the housekeeper. 'I often think Mrs Waverley has the right of it. Men! Wenching and carousing and boozing and getting the pox and preaching morality. Tchah!'

She put an arm about the weeping girl and helped her from the room.

The next day Mr Fordyce accepted delivery of a brand new brassbound telescope mounted on a stand and had it placed at the first floor window. He put a stool in front of it and focused it on the windows of Lady Artemis's drawing room. He knew that she had a similar telescope, but he was surprised to see her sitting peering through it. For one moment it appeared to him as if his magnified eye was staring straight into the magnified eye of Lady Artemis. He left the telescope and walked away in confusion. When a servant arrived with a note from Lady Artemis some ten minutes later, Mr Fordyce was almost frightened to open it in case she was accusing him of spying on her, for that is what he *had* been doing and why he had bought the telescope in the first place. 'Dear Friend,' he read, 'Come Quickly. I am in sore Distress, Yrs. A.V.'

His heart beating hard, Mr Fordyce shouted for his valet, changed into his best coat, brushed cologne on his hair and eyebrows, and hurried across the square, trying not to break into a run.

He was ushered into Lady Artemis's drawing room. She came to meet him, both hands outstretched. 'I am a monster,' she cried, and flung herself against him. Mr Fordyce patted her shoulder and murmured soothing rubbish in her ear – she was his pet, his darling, the most beautiful woman in the world.

At last she raised a tear-stained face. 'How can I aid you?' asked Mr Fordyce. 'You must not cry so.'

'I am in disgrace with Lord Tredair,' said Lady Artemis. 'You must help me regain his affection.'

Poor Mr Fordyce. All in that moment, he hated his best friend with a passion.

'I will do what I can,' he said stiffly. 'But surely you are mistaken.'

Lady Artemis sat down on the sofa and patted the space beside her. 'Come next to me,' she said, 'and I will tell you all.'

As Mr Fordyce listened, Lady Artemis told him about how she had gossiped and ruined the Waverley girls' reputations.

Mr Fordyce controled his burning desire to take her in his arms and kiss her breathless. He said, 'I think Mrs Waverley meant you to spread that scurrilous gossip.'

'But why?'

'She wants to keep them all to herself. Until recently they went nowhere but round the square for walks. She hates men and despises them. Tredair looks interested in Miss Fanny, so Tredair and all other threatening men must be kept at bay.'

'But now Tredair despises me for gossiping. What am I to do?'

Mr Fordyce thought quickly. He thought so hard and fast he could practically feel his mind jumping through hoops like those performing dogs at Astley's Amphitheatre. If only Tredair could marry Fanny, then Tredair would no longer be a rival.

'The first thing,' he said slowly, 'is to gossip about Mrs Waverley, to ruin *her* reputation by putting it about she lies about her girls so as to keep the men away. Let me think . . . and the reason she does this is to . . . is to . . . ah, I have it! . . . is to keep all suitors away because although the girls are not her daughters, they are of noble birth and each holds an enormous dowry. Make her hatred of men a joke.'

Lady Artemis twisted the fringe of her stole in her fingers. 'Do you think that would answer? I confess to a certain admiration for Mrs Waverley. She talks a great deal of sense.'

'About men being dreadful beasts?'

'No-o. But about it being a man's world and us the underdogs, the lap dogs of society, she calls us. A woman should be able to court a man, just as a man is able to court a woman.'

'But women do do that,' said Mr Fordyce with a fond smile, 'in their pretty little ways.'

'Like a dog standing on its hindlegs for attention,' said Lady Artemis. 'Now if I were to say to you, I wish to kiss you, Mr Fordyce, you would be alarmed and back away and put me down in your mind as a forward woman.'

'Try me,' said Mr Fordyce.

'Very well,' said Lady Artemis, beginning to look amused. 'Kiss me, Mr Fordyce.'

She looked at him with laughter in her eyes, expecting him to be embarrassed.

He seized her in his arms and kissed her passionately, kissed her as he had dreamed of kissing her since he first set eyes on her. She let out a mumble of protest but his lips were insistent, searching, passionate, his body now pressed against her own was throbbing and pulsating. Her own body began to respond, and she kissed him languorously back. Clasped together they slowly rolled off the sofa onto the floor.

At one point Lady Artemis surfaced briefly from

the sea of passion to wonder why such a normally correct and shy young man should be writhing on top of her now naked body, his own naked from the waist down, but with his coat still on, his waistcoat and his cravat as impeccable as it had been when he arrived.

At last, she lay lax and sated under him. Her hands slid over his naked bottom and she sighed. It had been so long. 'We must dress,' she said. 'What are you doing?'

For Mr Fordyce was urgently tearing off the rest of his clothes. He had a neat trim muscular body, now totally naked as he bent over her again.

'Mr Fordyce!' exclaimed Lady Artemis. 'You cannot possibly . . . I have not had breakfast. Oh, Mr Fordyce . . . !' Her voice faded away as he energetically rode her protests into extinction in an orgy of lovemaking on her drawing room carpet.

By midafternoon the happy couple were finally redressed, engaged to be married, and plotting ways to restore the Waverley girls' reputation. Any desire for Lord Tredair had faded completely from Lady Artemis's mind, but she still had a guilty conscience and was anxious to make amends.

'I will drive out on my calls,' she said sleepily, 'and start to gossip. I suggest you do the same and start in the clubs. But I must do more. I shall then call on Mrs Waverley again. If she thinks her girls' reputation is utterly ruined, then perhaps she may take them to the theater again or some such place she considers educational.'

'My love, before I gossip, I am going to get a special license and put a notice in all the newspapers of our betrothal.'

'Not yet,' said Lady Artemis, shaking her head.

'But why?'

'She is a disciple of Mary Wollstonecraft. That woman finally got married, if you remember, and disappointed all her acolytes who felt she had betrayed them. Silly, because the wigeon was as much in thrall to any man by simply living with him and bearing his children. Let me arrange something and then we will tell the world.'

'You promise?'

'I promise,' said Lady Artemis, stretching like a cat. 'Oh, I promise.'

But it was the next day before Lady Artemis felt strong enough to call on Mrs Waverley. All her guilty conscience returned as she sensed the sadness in the Waverley mansion. She did not know it, but although the brooch had been returned, Felicity and Frederica were worried about Fanny who trailed about, looking half alive.

Mrs Waverley received Lady Artemis. She was bored and was looking forward to resuming her teaching. 'I myself can attend, dear Mrs Waverley,' said Lady Artemis, 'but I fear you have disgraced yourself, and I might be the only lady prepared to come here.'

'I?' said Mrs Waverley awfully. 'How so?'

'You told us of the sad background of your girls but . . . er . . . someone talked.'

'Tut tut,' said Mrs Waverley complacently. 'But why am *I* in disgrace?'

'Well, to be sure, society thinks you are monstrously cruel to have betrayed them so. For had you kept quiet, society would have believed them to be your daughters.'

Mrs Waverley waved a fat hand dismissively. 'No matter. We do not go out.'

Lady Artemis looked at her slyly. 'Exactly,' she murmured. 'The *mad* Mrs Waverley.'

'*Mad?*'

'Oh, yes,' said Lady Artemis sweetly. 'Quite, quite mad. What has she to fear, they ask. How can someone of such strong principles fear the world so much? In fact, they are now saying you lied about your girls so that they would be tied to you for life and never leave you.'

'What nonsense!'

'But, of course, if you were to give them the lie . . .'

'How?'

'By taking the girls about. They need not go to balls and parties. There are plenty of educational interests in London. There is the museum with the Elgin marbles.'

'I do not care what society thinks.'

'Oh, but you should,' said Lady Artemis. 'No one is prepared to listen to the views of a woman they consider maliciously mad.'

'I do not believe you,' panted Mrs Waverley.

'Then send out cards again to one of your soirées. Even your own friends will not attend.'

'Please leave me,' said Mrs Waverley. 'You are talking nonsense.'

The next day she sent out cards to her friends, Miss Pursy, Miss Baxter, and Miss Dunbar. All sent replies refusing to attend and offering no apology.

Now Mrs Waverley had all the isolation she thought she had craved. She tried to console herself with the girls' company at dinner, but Fanny was wan and silent and Felicity and Frederica quietly angry about something.

'I cannot stand this atmosphere!' Mrs Waverley burst out at last. 'Have I not given you everything? My love, my home, my riches?'

The Waverley girls remained silent.

'Speak, I command you!'

Frederica looked at her and said coldly, 'You told the whole of London we were foundlings and bastards. May we know your reasons for doing so?'

'I only told someone in confidence. I did not mean any harm.'

'If you wish us to shun men,' said Frederica, still in that icy voice, 'then let us have freedom of choice. You say women are little better than slaves, and yet you have bound us more into slavery than any married drudge.'

'That is not true!'

'Oh, yes it is,' cried Felicity. 'What is our life to be now? You must tell everyone you lied. And then you must allow us to go out like the free women we should be. If you do not, then people will say you are a mad eccentric.'

156

This was exactly what Lady Artemis had said. Mrs Waverley began to cry noisily, occasionally peering through the hands, which covered her face, in the hope of seeing any softening in the three pairs of hard eyes that looked at her.

'What am I to do?' she said at last.

'You will go about on calls,' said Frederica firmly, 'and you will tell everyone that some jealous cat spread lies about us, and that we are, in fact, your real daughters. Only Lord Tredair will know that not to be the case.' She flicked a glance at Fanny. 'I suggest you summon him here and tell him to keep his mouth shut.'

'I cannot do it,' said Mrs Waverley, desperately trying to regain control. 'We are happy as we are.'

'Look at us,' commanded Frederica, her voice dripping with contempt. 'You have pushed us too far. We are now prepared to throw ourselves on the mercy of that orphanage, but before we do, we shall blacken your name in London so much that the mob will throw stones at your windows.'

'And,' said Felicity dreamily, 'they may even drag you out in the street and stone you, too.'

'Unnatural, unfeeling monsters!' screamed Mrs Waverley.

Fanny stood up. Of the three, she was the hardest, the most bitter. 'You have until tomorrow,' she said. 'And do not ever write letters and say they came from me again.'

'You have been seeing Tredair behind my back!' howled Mrs Waverley.

'Yes, I have. But if it is any comfort to you, he despises me and does not wish to see me again.'

Silently, the Waverley girls left the room. Mrs Waverley sobbed and yelled, occasionally tilting her head to one side to listen in the hope that just one would return to comfort her. But no one did.

NINE

Great waves of gossip about the Waverley girls pounded the shores of society. They were not bastards, they were Mrs Waverley's legitimate daughters. They were some noble lord's by-blows. Mrs Waverley had tried to glamorize herself by lying about them. They were fabulously rich and even when they sat down to breakfast, they were dripping with jewels.

Lady Artemis had a box at the opera and by nagging and manipulating, she persuaded Mrs Waverley to accept her invitation and bring the girls along.

Mrs Waverley was secretly eager to find out that no damage had been done. And when they reached Lady Artemis's box, such seemed to be the case. All sorts of people crowded the box, asking for introductions. For the one piece of gossip that had really stuck, was that the Waverleys were fabulously rich, and that idea of riches drew even the highest sticklers like moths to a flame.

'I told you I should make things come right,' whispered Mrs Waverley to Fanny after the second interval, but Fanny turned her head away and did not reply.

The earl was in the box opposite. Mr Fordyce, who was escorting them as well as Lady Artemis, had waved to his friend several times, but the earl merely nodded and did not make any attempt to come and join them.

Lady Artemis stole anxious little glances at Fanny's sad face. She herself was wildly happy. She no longer saw Mr Fordyce as a rather pleasant young man of no significant income, but as a powerful Adonis. And like most people in love, she wanted everyone around her to be happy.

The Waverleys unlike everyone else, were not attending the ball that always followed the opera. Mr Fordyce and Lady Artemis walked down the stairs with them to escort them to their carriage. They met the Earl of Tredair. He smiled warmly at Mr Fordyce and Lady Artemis, nodded coldly to Mrs Waverley, glanced with contempt at Fanny, who blushed miserably and looked away, and ignored the other two girls completely.

'Now I feel really wretched,' said Lady Artemis later at the ball, wondering how she could ever have chased after such a cold, haughty fish as the earl. 'Did you not mark the way Tredair looked at poor Fanny? I felt ready to sink. I am surprised he should be so high in the instep. He obviously still believes all that gossip about her birth. There must be something I can do.'

'Leave him to me,' said Mr Fordyce, pressing her hand. 'And I am afraid he is the one who has absolute proof that the gossip is true.'

He decided to visit the earl on the morrow and see if he could learn the reason for Tredair's sudden disgust of Fanny.

He knew he would probably find the earl at White's at eleven in the morning. The earl liked to settle down in the coffee room at that time while the rest of the members stayed at home and slept off the memory of their gambling losses.

The earl looked up as Mr Fordyce approached him and smiled lazily. 'How goes your pursuit of Lady Artemis?'

'Successful. You may congratulate me!'

'Then I do. When is the wedding to take place?'

'As soon as possible.'

The earl fought down a qualm of unease. He thought Mr Fordyce was much too good for Lady Artemis. He remembered his own harsh words to Lady Artemis.

'And when is the betrothal to be announced?' he asked.

'Well, that's just it,' said Mr Fordyce. 'My beloved is all heart.'

The earl felt his own eyebrows rise cynically, but pulled them down into place and adopted an air of polite interest.

'We cannot announce anything until we are sure all is well with the Waverley girls,' said Mr Fordyce.

The earl's face hardened. 'I do not see that the affairs of that odd household should stop you putting an announcement in the newspapers.'

'Lady Artemis is bitterly ashamed of the damage she did by gossiping about them at that breakfast.'

'You amaze me,' said the earl.

'She feels if the betrothal is announced, Mrs Waverley will no longer grant her admittance. Mrs Waverley belongs to the brand of bluestocking that believes marriage a betrayal of their sex.'

'Since she herself has had the experience of marriage, you would think she would leave her sex free to find out for themselves.'

'Be that as it may,' said Mr Fordyce eagerly, 'Lady Artemis is first anxious to see if she can persuade Mrs Waverley into allowing the girls more freedom.'

'Then it was she,' said the earl, 'who obviously manipulated Mrs Waverley into taking them all to the opera last night!'

'Yes, and my poor Verity should have been in high alt, but she was cast down.'

'Really,' said the earl in a bored voice.

'Do you not wish to know why?'

'Of course,' lied the earl.

'She cannot bear to see the distress of Miss Fanny, and she noticed your savage coldness toward the girl.'

'My savage . . . . ? You have been reading too many novels. If I remember, I was all that was polite.'

'You were very frosty, and you glared at Miss Fanny so. I am surprised at you. Even if the girl is a foundling, there is no reason to take her in dislike. She is not responsible for her birth.'

'Let me say I am not angry with Miss Fanny because of her birth. There is something else . . .'

Mr Fordyce hitched his chair forward and stared eagerly at the earl like a dog waiting for a bone.

The earl tapped his fingers on the arm of his chair. He was about to say he would not discuss it. But he was longing to talk about it. He felt he had behaved commendably, and yet there was a niggling seed of doubt.

'If I tell you, you must promise not to tell anyone, particularly Lady Artemis.'

'I promise,' said Mr Fordyce and crossed his fingers behind his back.

'Miss Fanny sent her housekeeper to seek me out,' said the earl. 'I was let into the servants hall to have an audience with her. She told me, and mark this well, that she had been in the habit of taking jewels and pawning them for pin money. One jewel, a brooch, remained to be redeemed and she had not the ready. She appealed to me to buy it back for her.'

'And?' prompted Mr Fordyce eagerly.

'And that's it,' said the earl crossly. 'I redeemed the brooch for her. She is a thief. There is bad blood there.'

Mr Fordyce leaned back in his chair and looked at the earl in consternation.

'Are the girls not allowed any pin money?'

'No.'

'Well, then . . .' began Mr Fordyce awkwardly. 'It stands to reason . . .'

'You are forgetting one salient fact. She is a thief.'

'But think of her unnatural life. No freedom. Kept indoors.'

'The girls, as you very well know, were in the habit of escaping by the garden of your house. There was no reason for them to steal from their benefactress.'

'They probably didn't see it that way,' pleaded Mr Fordyce. 'They probably thought they were just borrowing it.'

'Indeed! And just how did they intend to find money to get back the items?'

'Well, you are very hard. Very hard indeed. They are taken out of the orphanage and immediately draped with jewels and trinkets. They are so used to jewels that they do not really seem more than baubles and toys to them.'

'They knew the value of them enough to pawn them.'

Mr Fordyce felt himself becoming very hot and angry. 'It is easy for you to be high and mighty,' he snapped. 'What if you yourself were in a situation where you wanted something and needed to steal to get it, would you not just take it?'

'Certainly not,' said the earl. He picked up his newspaper and rustled the pages.

'It is of no use talking to you,' said Mr Fordyce, rising to take his leave.

'On that particular matter, none whatsoever,' said the earl.

Mr Fordyce went straight to Lady Artemis and blurted out the whole thing. 'Well, to be sure it is bad in one way,' said Lady Artemis, 'but under the circumstances, the whole house is an invitation to theft. Mrs Waverley often leaves brooches and necklaces lying around. If the girls were so very bad, they could gain their freedom by simply taking the contents of their jewel boxes and disappearing to the continent where they could live in luxury for the rest of their lives.'

'But Tredair is so hard, so adamant. I did not know he was such a cruel and unfeeling man.'

Mr Fordyce was always anxious to put down his friend, for he had a lurking fear that Lady Artemis might become enamored of the earl again.

'Not like you,' she whispered, leaning toward him. His hands reached blindly for her, and soon they were busily engaged in their favorite sport.

The earl continued to read the newspapers, all of them, from cover to cover with great concentration. Fanny's face had an irritating way of rising up between him and the printed word, but nonetheless he persevered. He was just perusing an advertisement that read, 'A Young Lady of Respectability is desirous of procuring a situation as Companion. She has a knowledge of dressmaking and is prepared to make herself useful in any way, non-menial,' when he was interrupted by old Lord Struthers, who poked the earl in the chest with his cane and said, 'Heard the news?'

'Take that cane away,' said the earl. 'What news?'

'The Marquess of Pilkington has just spoken in the Lords.'

'The Marquess of Pilkington is always speaking in the Lords.'

'But he caused a sensation. Did you know he was a foundling?'

'No. He has always been regarded as the eldest son of the Duke and Duchess of Hadshire.'

'Exactly. But it transpires they adopted him. This damn Waverley woman everyone's gossiping about has touched him on the raw. He made a powerful speech. He said a wretched woman, he referred to her as Mrs W., had tried to ruin the reputation of her charges by telling the world they were foundlings and so trying to puff herself up by appearing a noble and charitable lady. "I am a foundling," booms Pilkington. "I was adopted! And yet, am I not an aristocrat? All this business about aristocratic blood and heredity traits is rubbish. It is upbringing and money that provide the bronze." He ranted on and then finished up by crying, "Let no one say that one Englishman is not as good as another." Of course, the Whigs in the lower house got to hear of it and when the old boy emerged, they took his horses away and pulled his chariot through the streets themselves, shouting, "Liberty! Equality!" '

The earl felt a sudden sick feeling of dread. 'Excuse me,' he muttered and ran from the club. He called at Mr Fordyce's house in Hanover Square. Mr Fordyce was not at home. The earl hurried across the square to Lady Artemis's house.

'Is Mr Fordyce here?' he shouted to the butler.

'Yes, my lord. In the drawing room. But, my lord
. . . !' The earl pushed past him, as the butler tried to
bar his way, and hurtled up the stairs and flung open
the double doors of the drawing room.

It was, he thought, as he quickly slammed the
doors shut again and stood with his face flaming, the
most complicated piece of sexual intercourse a man
had ever been unlucky enough to witness.

'I tried to tell you, my lord,' said the butler gloomily. 'I tried to warn you.'

The earl made his way back down the stairs. But
the drawing room doors opened and Mr Fordyce,
now decently clad in a dressing gown, popped his
head out. 'Thought it was you,' he called. 'What's
amiss?'

'Come down here, man, and I'll tell you,' said the
earl.

Mr Fordyce pattered down the stairs in his bare
feet and led the way into a salon off the main hall.

'I am sorry I burst in on you,' said the earl, 'but the
matter was most urgent.'

'Don't mention it,' said Mr Fordyce airily. 'Lady
Artemis didn't see you. Thought it was one of the
servants. No need to upset her.'

'The fact is this. I need your help and Lady
Artemis's help to persuade Mrs Waverley to remove
herself from town and quickly too.'

'Why?'

'I should think the mob will be around to attack
her any moment now.' He told Mr Fordyce of the

marquess's speech in the House of Lords. 'So, don't you see,' finished the earl, 'this is just the sort of excuse the mob needs for looting and burning.'

The earl waited until Lady Artemis and Mr Fordyce got dressed. Soon the three were hurrying across the square to the Waverley mansion, the earl glancing at the sedate couple beside him and trying to banish that picture of them in the drawing room from his mind. He wondered where his friend had got the idea from. The frescoes at Pompeii?

Mrs Waverley was in her drawing room with the three girls when Mrs Ricketts introduced Lady Artemis, Mr Fordyce, and the earl.

Before Mrs Waverley could start to protest about the unheralded visit, the earl succinctly outlined the problem.

Mrs Waverley tossed her head. 'I shall not run before the mob,' she said, her eyes flashing.

Frederica cast a rather malicious look in the direction of Mrs Waverley and asked, 'Is the mob going to tear us all to pieces?'

'No,' said the earl. 'They regard you girls in the light of heroines. It is Mrs Waverley's blood they are after.'

'Good,' murmured Frederica, and picked up her sewing again.

Mrs Waverley turned a muddy color. 'You are exaggerating, my lord.'

'Not I. I should estimate you have a bare half hour in which to escape.'

Mrs Waverley's defences crumpled. 'But where?' she wailed. 'Where can we go?'

'I have a very pretty house at Brighton,' said Lady Artemis. 'We shall all travel there.'

'Good,' said the earl. 'I shall send you on your way.'

Lady Artemis and Mr Fordyce exchanged glances. 'Better come with us,' said Mr Fordyce. 'You can't abandon us. The ladies may need protection on the road.'

The earl nodded reluctantly and began to rap out orders.

Fanny stuffed clothes and jewels into a trunk, her heart beating hard. She tried to tell herself that her excitement was at the prospect of escaping from London and nothing to do with seeing the earl again.

The earl's servants, summoned by one of Mrs Waverley's housemaids, arrived as well and the whole house was in an uproar. It was a full hour before three heavily laden carriages moved out of the square. All around Hanover Square, the houses already stood shuttered. The news of a possible attack by the mob had gone around the square like wildfire.

Mrs Waverley sat in the carriage as it moved off, white and shaken. She could only be glad amidst all her distress that the Earl of Tredair had not once looked at Fanny.

Fanny, Frederica, and Felicity were content to watch the passing scene. Each was silently blessing the mob. They were to see Brighton. They were to stay in Lady Artemis's house where surely Mrs Waverley could not have a say in how things were done. Lady Artemis was frivolous and would want to entertain. Fanny thought about how Lady Artemis and Mr Fordyce kept gazing into each other's eyes. They were obviously very much in love. She remembered how she had thought she loved the earl. She must have been weak in the head. That haughty aristocrat would not stay in Brighton very long. He would disassociate himself from such unfashionable company as soon as possible. Fanny wrenched her mind away from the earl. She would be able to visit circulating libraries and walk about the shops, and she would look upon the ocean for the first time.

Mrs Waverley's heartbeats slowed to a regular pace as the miles between them and London grew longer. She had no intention of residing very long with Lady Artemis. She herself would find a house to rent and take her precious girls with her before they became too accustomed to the pernicious and frivolous ways of society.

In another coach Lady Artemis and Mr Fordyce swayed companionably together with the movement of the carriage. 'What are we to do about Tredair and Fanny?' asked Lady Artemis.

'You know, my love,' said Mr Fordyce, 'he is not a free spirit like us. Quite a Puritan. I think we should forget about them and get married as soon as possible.'

'I would like to see him knocked from his high horse,' said Lady Artemis. 'I would like to take him somewhere far away and steal all his money so that he had to thieve to get something to eat.'

The earl was driving his own coach, sitting up on the box, wrapped in gloomy thought. He thought it infuriating that Fanny's downcast face should make *him* feel so guilty. Here he was involved with eccentrics and he detested eccentrics. He had refused an invitation to Lord Wirt's the other week. Everyone else who had been invited was eager to go because Lord Wirt never saw his guests but lived in a sort of corridor between the walls of his mansion and spoke to visitors through a small aperture. The earl detested such odd behavior and thought that people who encouraged it by visiting the old freak were just as bad. Now he was stuck with Mrs Waverley, whom he damned as being the worst type of eccentric.

Lady Artemis's Brighton house faced the sea. Dinner that evening was supplied by a nearby hotel. It should have been a merry party, thought Lady Artemis bitterly, had it not been for that old frump, Waverley. The girls were beside themselves with excitement at their first view of the sea and had begged to be able to go out, but that lady had refused point blank. Not only that, instead of expressing herself in flattering terms of gratitude to her hostess for her rescue, she had said she would go out on the morrow to find a house of her own.

At last, it was all too much. The girls were picking at their food. Lord Tredair's face looked as if it had been carved out of stone. Lady Artemis excused herself and went up to her bedroom and ferreted in a large medicine chest until she found what she was looking for.

Mrs Waverley had insisted the girls drink nothing stronger than lemonade. Lady Artemis handed a sachet of powder to her butler and told him to mix it in a glass of lemonade and hand it to Mrs Waverley. She also handed the butler a guinea to wipe the look of consternation from his face.

Lady Artemis saw the butler hand the glass of lemonade to a footman who placed it in front of Mrs Waverley.

Mrs Waverley was prosing on, quoting that bore Wollstonecraft. 'The man,' intoned Mrs Waverley, 'who can be contented to live with a pretty, useful companion, without a mind, has lost in voluptuous gratifications a taste for more refined enjoyment. He has never felt the calm satisfaction that refreshes the parched heart, like the silent dew of heaven, of being beloved by one who could understand him. He . . .'

Lady Artemis leapt to her feet. 'Ladies, gentlemen,' she cried. 'I give you a toast. The King.'

Everyone rose to their feet and raised their glasses. 'The King!' Mrs Waverley took a sip from her lemonade and made to sit down. 'And the Queen!' said Lady Artemis. The queen's health was duly drunk. 'And the Prince Regent,' said Lady Artemis desperately. Sip, sip went Mrs Waverley. 'The rights of woman!' called Lady Artemis. Mrs Waverley beamed and drained her glass.

'As I was saying,' began Mrs Waverley again, 'women are kept from the tree of knowledge . . .

the rational hopes of women are to be sacrificed to render women an object of desire for a short time. Women . . .'

Her voice trailed away and she put a hand to her head. 'Excuse me. I feel dizzy. The journey.'

'Girls!' said Lady Artemis. 'Mrs Waverley is ill. Assist her to her room.'

Mrs Waverley was a heavy woman. It took all the energies of the Waverley girls and two footmen to get her up the stairs.

By the time the girls had returned, the lemonade had disappeared to be replaced by champagne.

Outside the sun was sinking lower over the sea. Lady Artemis saw the wistful look Fanny cast at the ocean and said gaily, 'I am sure you young ladies would benefit from a brisk walk before bedtime. Do put on warm wraps for the wind has become chilly.'

'You had better escort them, Tredair,' said Lady Artemis. 'My poor Mr Fordyce is feeling faint as well.'

She pressed Mr Fordyce's foot under the table in warning as he opened his mouth to protest.

'Very well,' said the earl with obvious reluctance. 'I shall go straight to bed on my return. I thank you now for your hospitality, Lady Artemis. I shall be gone to London in the morning by the time you rise.'

'And that's that,' said Lady Artemis when they had all gone. 'I could shake him. Just look at those girls!'

The Waverley girls were running up and down the shingle, dodging the waves. The earl was sitting moodily on a rock watching them.

'I don't think he cares for Fanny,' said Mr Fordyce.

'Oh, he does. I am sure of it. I want her to be happy. I only gossipped to spite her, you know. I did not know then I should love you.'

'Well, at least Miss Fanny has a little moment of freedom,' said Mr Fordyce. 'How convenient Mrs Waverley fell ill.'

'Stoopid! I drugged her.'

'I say!'

'Do you know what I would like to do?' said Lady Artemis dreamily. 'I would like to drug Tredair and Fanny and take them far away to . . . Oh, I know, my aunt has a house several miles from here up on the downs, quite isolated, and she is abroad at the moment. I would leave them there and take all Tredair's money and force him to find his own way back. I would leave money in the house so that he would have to take it to get them home.'

'He would think nothing of that. He would drive back out as soon as he had deposited Fanny and pay the money back.'

'But they would be thrown together, don't you see? Something would have to happen. He would be compromised.'

'He would know we had drugged him.'

'He couldn't prove it.'

'You are as mad as Mrs Waverley.'

Lady Artemis began to cry. 'If you loved me, you would help me.'

'My sweet. Anything. Only don't cry.'

Mr Fordyce hugged her and caressed her, confident

174

that she would forget all this crazy nonsense after a good night's sleep.

'Psst!'

Mr Fordyce started awake.

'It is I,' whispered Lady Artemis. 'Get your clothes on, my love. We have work to do.'

'Certainly,' said Mr Fordyce cheerfully, jerking her on top of him and fumbling with the tapes of her gown.

'Not that!' she said, slapping at his hands. 'I have drugged Tredair and Fanny. Now we have to move them to my aunt's house.'

'Tredair's a big man. How are we supposed to carry him out? We cannot manage him between us.'

'My servants will do the work. They have been told it is a practical joke and have been paid to keep their mouths shut. Do come along, my love.'

Had he been less besotted, then Mr Fordyce would have refused. But he felt as drugged with love as their victims were with sleeping powders.

It all went like a dream. The heaving of the bodies into Lady Artemis's traveling carriage, the ride through the night, the grunts of the servants as they struggled with the bodies at the other end. 'Get the key,' hissed Lady Artemis to Mr Fordyce. 'It's in the gutter.'

Mr Fordyce felt along the gutter until his fingers encountered a key. He took it down and opened the door.

'Do we dump them in bed together?' he asked.

'That would be quite shocking,' said Lady Artemis primly. 'See, there are two easy chairs, one on either side of the fire. Place them one in each chair. Now, I shall leave money on the table. We will lock them in so that they can have an adventurous time trying to escape. La! I hope these powders were not too strong. I don't want them to sleep forever. Have the fire made up so they do not freeze and put blankets over them. Good!'

Mr Fordyce performed the duties allotted to him. It all seemed like such a good joke. He and Lady Artemis giggled like schoolchildren when they finally crept out after the servants and locked the door and took away the key.

One of the servants drove back, while Lady Artemis and Mr Fordyce traveled inside, hugging and kissing and laughing.

The cottage was some twenty miles outside Brighton, so it was dawn by the time they reached home.

As he undressed for bed, Mr Fordyce wondered sleepily whether the earl would call him out, but then Tredair could hardly do that, provided they all kept to the story that the house had been broken into during the night and that Fanny and the earl had for some cruel and mysterious reason been abducted.

He did not awake until two o'clock the following afternoon. The events of the night came rushing back to him and he clutched his hair.

Tredair would not believe one word of that rubbish about abduction. Tredair would kill him!

He scrambled into his clothes and rode like a fury for the house where he had left Tredair and Fanny.

The door was lying splintered on the front path.

There was no one inside.

The earl and Fanny had gone.

TEN

The earl stretched and yawned. He slowly opened his eyes. At first he did not think he was awake but merely moving into a strange dream. He saw the sleeping figure of Fanny in an armchair opposite, clad only in her nightgown. He twisted his head and looked vaguely around at the cottage parlor. Then he looked down at his own body, at his nightshirt and bare feet. He moved one foot and struck his toe against a footstool. With dawning horror, he realized he was not in a dream.

He got to his feet, nearly banging his head on the rafters, and went out of the room into the vestibule and tried the outside door. Locked!

He shook his head to clear it.

Trickery and treachery, he thought bitterly. What a fool he had been to believe all that nonsense about Mrs Waverley trying to stop him marrying Fanny.

All the while she had been plotting and scheming. She must have been afraid he might change his mind because of Fanny's birth, and so this was her way of making sure he would *have* to marry Fanny.

He walked back into the parlor, leaned down, and shook Fanny roughly by the shoulder. 'Wake up!' he shouted.

Fanny groggily came awake. Her eyes widened when she saw the earl standing over her in his night-shirt. 'Where are we? What are you doing here? How did I get here?' she cried. She tried to get to her feet, and then sat down again with a groan. 'I feel sick,' she said, 'and my throat is dry.'

'We have both been drugged,' said the earl. 'I do not know where we are, but wherever it is, we are locked in without our clothes.'

'Were we attacked?' asked Fanny. 'The mob . . . Fanny, Frederica . . . Mrs Waverley? Are they all right?'

'The facts appear to be this,' he said. 'Your Mrs Waverley, far from trying to stop me marrying you, has plotted and planned to make sure I do so. Well, I shall not be coerced into marrying you. I shall . . .'

'Mrs Waverley would never do such a thing,' said Fanny. 'Never! But Lady Artemis would.'

'Why?'

'Sheer, simple spite,' said Fanny furiously. 'Painted useless trollop. I could kill her.'

'I do not believe you,' he said, striding up and down with his hands clasped behind his back. 'This

179

is what comes of women holding unnatural views. This is . . .'

'Shut up,' said Fanny crossly. 'If you are going to be pompous, wait until you have some clothes on. I have been drugged, I am cold, I am thirsty, and I am not going to put up with a jaw-me-dead from a man in a nightshirt.'

'You are right,' he said with a sudden grin. 'How sad that I should look ridiculous in my nightwear and you should look so enchanting.'

'It is no time for empty compliments either,' said Fanny briskly. 'Whoever played this trick must be confounded. I have no intention of marrying you. I already have no reputation to speak of, and I can live down this scandal. It is only women who hope to marry who must worry about their reputations. Where is the kitchen?'

'I do not know, madam. I have had a lot more to think about than . . .'

'Men!' Fanny got to her feet and went out into the little vestibule. She rattled the outside door and then turned about and went back into the parlor then through a door at the back that led to a kitchen that had obviously been built on as a recent extension. Through the kitchen window, she could see a pump standing in the yard. At that moment the hardest thing to bear, as far as Fanny was concerned, was having to stand in that kitchen with a raging thirst and not be able to get a drink of water.

The earl had followed her in and was trying the back door. 'Locked and stronger than the front,' he said.

Fanny wordlessly pushed past him and went upstairs. There were two bedrooms with dormer windows set into the thatch. There was a chest on the floor of the one that had obviously been used the most. She threw open the lid and found a pile of old gowns. She was just selecting one of the gowns, when the earl came in to join her.

'You seem to have found what you need,' he said. 'Any men's clothes?'

'Try the other bedroom,' said Fanny curtly. 'That is, if you don't mind stealing.'

'This is not stealing. This is necessity.'

'Oh, it's always different for you,' said Fanny.

'May I point out that I am imprisoned?'

'Like I usually am,' said Fanny. 'Go away and do something useful. My head hurts.'

Fanny found a pair of flat-heeled shoes in a cupboard. They were a trifle large, but she lashed the ribbons tightly around her ankles to secure them. The gown she had put on was of expensive material, but old-fashioned in cut and smelled strongly of camphor. She had also found a shift and stockings in a chest of drawers. There was a toilet table in one corner laden with jars of creams and pomatums. The water jug was empty.

'Found anything?' she called to the earl.

'Yes,' he replied. 'I shall be with you presently.'

Fanny sat down at the toilet table and picked up a brush and brushed her hair and then braided it into a coronet on top of her head.

The nausea she had felt on waking had gone, but

181

the raging thirst was still there. She was just thinking of all the nasty things she would like to do to Lady Artemis when the earl came in.

Fanny stifled a snort of laughter. 'What clothes!' she said. 'You look like a peasant beau of the 1790s!'

The earl was wearing a tight-waisted coat with very long tails. The ruffled shirt, which showed at his throat, was slightly yellow with age. He had on a striped waistcoat and yellowish-white breeches and boots. 'The boots fit,' he said, 'but that is all that does fit. Whoever lived here was a lady to judge by the quality of your clothes, and to judge by the quality of mine, she once had a very low and shabby beau in residence. But the soles of these boots are quite thick. If I cannot force the front door with my shoulder, at least I can kick it down.'

They went down the stairs again. The earl was getting tired of having to walk with his head bent to avoid hitting it on the ceiling.

Fanny went back into the parlor. 'There's money on the table here,' she called over her shoulder. 'Good, we can take it and walk to the nearest place and hire a gig.'

'Leave it,' said the earl. 'I will not take anyone else's money – something that is hard, I know, for you to understand.'

'It is Lady Artemis's money!' shouted Fanny.

'It probably belongs to whomever owns this cottage. It is one thing to borrow a few old clothes, quite another to take money.'

'You know,' said Fanny in conversational tones,

'you are a very silly man. I am glad we are not to be married. What a cold and pompous fish you have turned out to be.'

'It is very hard to try to explain morals and right and wrong to someone who is amoral,' he snapped.

'If you were not in such a childish rage, you would take the money, but you are determined to make me feel bad about taking that jewelry,' said Fanny. 'Don't worry. I still feel wretched about that.'

He went back out of the parlor and looked at the front door. He thought of the trick that had been played on them. He kicked at the lock with savage force. There was a splintering sound as the lock gave. He continued to take his rage out on the door, kicking now at the hinges. Then he flung his weight against it and the whole door fell off its hinges onto the garden path and the earl with it.

Fanny walked delicately around his prone body and disappeared around the side of the cottage. He got to his feet and went after her. She was energetically operating the pump handle in the back yard.

'Let me,' he said, shouldering her aside. Soon a jet of clear water came pouring out, Fanny cupped her hands under it and drank and drank and then splashed water over her face.

While the earl washed his face, she looked about her. It was a sunny morning. A lark soared up into the clear air from the fields behind the cottage. The air was full of the smell of honeysuckle and roses from the tangle of the neglected garden.

Fanny took a deep breath and began to counsel

herself. 'You are safe and well, Fanny Waverley, and all we have to do is find a village. Now, do I take that money? No, I cannot. He will jeer at me and call me thief.'

'I suggest we set out immediately,' said the earl.

She looked so pretty, standing there in the sunlight, that he began to feel he had been behaving like a bear. It was not her fault that they were in this situation. Once again, he was amazed at her courage. She had been drugged and abducted and placed in a humiliating position, and yet she had neither screamed nor fainted.

He looked at her with a certain amount of tenderness in his eyes. Fanny saw that look and somehow it made her angrier than all his insults.

'If we are going, let us go,' she said sharply. 'You do look so utterly ridiculous in those clothes, I find it hard not to laugh.'

'Very well, Miss Fanny,' he said, turning about.

'Are you not going to take the money?' she said, falling into step beside him as they reached the road.

'No,' he said. 'It is a fine day and we will soon be rescued.'

It certainly looked as if their rescue was to be quickly at hand. They had only walked about half a mile when they saw a smart gig coming along the road toward them. In it sat what seemed like a prosperous-looking farmer and his wife. The earl hailed them.

The farmer reined in his horse and eyed them with disfavor. His plump wife clutched the reticule in her lap even tighter.

'I say, fellow,' said the earl in his lazy drawl. 'We are anxious to get to Brighton. Can you take us up?'

The earl's manner and voice, which would have been quite in keeping with his normal appearance, seemed like sheer impertinence to the farmer who only saw a jackanapes in the clothes of a shabby dandy.

'Brighton's the other way,' said the farmer. Brighton was actually in the direction the farmer was going, but he wanted shot of this odd and sinister pair.

'My name is Tredair,' said the earl. The farmer looked at him blankly. 'Lord Tredair,' said the earl. 'If you will take us at least a little way along the road, say to the nearest village, you will be handsomely rewarded.'

'Stand out of my way,' growled the farmer, raising his whip. Now he knew this man to be a villain. What lord ever wore such clothes?

The earl stood back in surprise. The farmer cracked his whip and the gig bowled past them. They both walked into the middle of the road and looked after it.

'Good gracious!' said the earl. 'What odd behavior. Why are you laughing in that idiotic way?'

'It's you,' giggled Fanny. 'You should see yourself. "I am Tredair," indeed. Of course he didn't believe you.'

The earl gave a reluctant grin. 'At least we know we are on the right road. I hope we come to somewhere soon, for I am sharp set.'

The couple smiled at each other in sudden

friendship. He held out his arm and Fanny took it. Together they strolled along the road, confident they would either soon see the buildings of Brighton across the downs, or at the very least, some sort of house and village.

But they walked and walked through the lazy, dusty sunshine without meeting anyone, without seeing a single house. Fanny's feet were beginning to ache. She stumbled once or twice, but when he offered to carry her, she refused.

And then at last, like a mirage, rising up among the dust and sunshine, they saw a trim country house set back from the road.

'Sanctuary!' said the earl, giving Fanny a quick hug. 'Come along. Breakfast and pots and pots of tea!'

With quickened footsteps they went up the short drive. The earl pounded at the knocker.

The door was opened by a thin, spare woman in a cap and apron who looked them up and down.

'No hawkers, no gypsies,' she said, and made to close the door. The earl put his foot in it to stop it closing, and the woman ran off into the house, screaming, 'Mr Digby! Mr Digby!'

'Is everyone quite mad?' said the earl testily. 'Come into the hall out of the heat, Fanny.'

'I feel like an intruder,' said Fanny, standing close beside him. A door at the far end of the hall opened and a man in clerical clothes, carrying a large horse pistol, came out and stood facing them.

'I am Mr Digby, the rector of the parish of St Paul,' he said. He leveled the pistol at the earl. 'Leave!'

'Mr Digby,' said the earl haughtily. 'My name is Tredair, the Earl of Tredair, and this is Miss Fanny Waverley.' The pistol remained pointed at him. 'Come, sir. Show some charity. We are tired and hungry.'

'What is an earl doing, wandering the countryside in such dreadful clothes?' said Mr Digby, who had a dry scholarly voice to match his thin scholarly face.

'We have had a dreadful trick played on us,' said the earl. 'We were both abducted and left locked in a cottage some distance from here. We were both in our night rail and had to borrow these old clothes from the cottage. If you will send a servant into Brighton with a letter from me, the matter can be straightened out.'

'Brighton is quite a distance away. I do not trust you, sir,' said the rector. 'You have the look of a highwayman about you.'

The earl would have stalked out had he been on his own, but pity for Fanny made him say, 'Can you please not give this lady something to eat and drink?'

Mr Digby studied them for what seemed an age. Then he slightly lowered the pistol. 'Although your appearance is villainous,' he said, 'I cannot find it in my heart to believe ill of your sweet lady. You are no doubt one of those villains of the road who drag some poor, loyal wife about with them on their nefarious thieving expeditions. Very well, you shall have food and drink . . . after you work for it.'

'What is this work?' demanded the earl, who was tired of protesting and arguing.

'You will find wood in the pinking shed that has not been blocked. There are three tree trunks, two to be blocked off, half of the other to be blocked, and the remaining chopped for kindling. While you get on with that, your lady may weed the flower beds.'

'Gladly,' said Fanny.

'The quicker you do it, then the quicker you will be fed,' said Mr Digby. 'But do not plague me any more with tales of earls, or I might change my mind. Every hale and hearty beggar who comes to my door must work for his charity. The lame, and sick, of course, do not need to do so.'

'I shall do the work for you,' said the earl crossly, 'but leave this lady to rest.'

'I see no reason why a perfectly healthy young woman should not earn her keep,' said Mr Digby.

'Quite right,' agreed Fanny.

Soon she was bent over the flower beds, busily weeding. Mr Digby had told her the gardener had been sick for some weeks and so the garden had become neglected. As she weeded, Mr Digby's words rang in her head. 'I see no reason why a perfectly healthy young woman should not earn her keep.' Fanny's mind raced. Even when the housekeeper briefly emerged to hand her a gardening hat, Fanny's plans and thoughts went racing on as her nimble fingers pulled out the weeds. She could find a post as a governess. The earl would surely help her to do that! Oh, to be free! No longer would she be dependent on Mrs Waverley. She would have her own money. Make her own life.

She was so busy with her thoughts that it came as a surprise when she heard Mr Digby and the earl approaching. Mr Digby was saying severely, 'You did that work in record time. What a waste of a life. Take my advice, young fellow, and apply yourself to a trade.'

'Come along, Fanny,' said the earl. 'We are to be fed at last.'

Fanny sighed with relief when they were led into a cool dark kitchen. The food was good and plentiful and there was even ale to go with it. The earl and Fanny ate and drank silently, each aware of the grim housekeeper, who stood watching them with her arms folded.

When they were finished, the earl said, 'If you will convey me to your master, my good woman, we will thank him.'

'Don't give me any of your hoity-toity airs,' said the housekeeper. 'Off with the pair of you and don't come around here again!'

She held open the kitchen door and jerked her head.

The earl was obviously about to protest, but Fanny tugged at his sleeve. 'Let's go,' she whispered. 'No one here is going to believe us if we talk and talk till Doomsday.'

The earl paused on the threshold, remembering that farmer, a sudden sharp suspicion crossing his mind.

'Which way is Brighton?' he asked the housekeeper.

'Turn left at the bottom of the drive and keep on going,' she said.

'Are you sure?' wailed Fanny. 'We have just come that way and we walked miles and miles.'

'That's the way to Brighton and that's the way it's always been,' said the housekeeper.

They wearily trudged down the drive.

'We had better go on the way we were going,' said the earl. 'Oh, here comes that tiresome woman again!'

The housekeeper came running after them. She reluctantly held out a guinea to Fanny. 'Master says you've to take this,' she said. 'Throwing away good money, I call it.'

'Thank him very much,' said Fanny quickly, for she feared the earl was going to refuse.

They walked out into the road.

'Since he is the rector, the church must be quite near,' said the earl, 'and where there's a church, there will be houses.'

Fanny stumbled and swayed, and he caught her in his arms.

'I'm sorry,' said Fanny weakly. 'It's the effect of the drug and the food and the sunshine. If I could just lie down for a few moments . . .'

'There's a field over there,' said the earl. 'We can lie in the shade of the hedge for a bit.'

He swung her up in his arms and carried her into the field. He lowered her gently onto the grass and then took off his coat and made it into a pillow and put it under her head. He lay down beside her and took her in his arms and cradled her against his chest.

'Sleep, Fanny,' he said. 'Look, I'm sorry for all the

hard things I said to you. I was a fool not to have taken that money from the cottage table.'

But Fanny was already asleep. He kissed her tenderly on the cheek and then fell asleep himself.

When Mr Fordyce had returned after failing to find the couple, he expected the house to be in an uproar. But Felicity and Frederica had assumed Fanny had escaped to go walking by the sea and so had lied to Mrs Waverley that she was lying down in her room, and the earl was assumed to be well on the road to London, Mr Fordyce having sent the earl's valet away, saying his master was waiting for him in town.

Mr Fordyce sought out Lady Artemis. 'I am terrified,' he said. 'We must have been mad. Tredair will be here at any moment, and he will either call me out or take both of us to court. You've no idea what he's like when he's in a rage.'

'I think I drank too much champagne last night,' said Lady Artemis. 'My love, perhaps it would be better if we moved back to London. Mrs Waverley can have the house. She will be glad to be shot of us, and she has her own servants here.'

'That is a cowardly action,' said Mr Fordyce. 'I think we should face Tredair together.'

'He will kill you,' pointed out Lady Artemis.

Felicity and Frederica watched anxiously as Lady Artemis and Mr Fordyce made hurried preparations for their departure. They were becoming increasingly worried over Fanny's disappearance.

When Lady Artemis and Mr Fordyce had finally

set out on the London road, both went to see Mrs Waverley and told that astounded and furious woman that Fanny had disappeared, leaving all her clothes and jewels behind.

'She has gone off with Tredair, you fools,' said Mrs Waverley. 'Did you not think of that?' She began to cry. 'Fanny is a wicked girl. Her name must never be mentioned in this house again. Never!'

'She would not go without leaving us a letter,' said Frederica stubbornly.

'She never cared for anyone but herself,' said Mrs Waverley passionately. 'She is a snake! A viper!'

Frederica and Felicity retreated quietly and went upstairs to one of the rooms that had a bay window overlooking the sea. They sat in silence, holding hands, and watching the sun sink lower in the sky. Neither could believe that Fanny was gone and would never return.

The earl awoke and looked up at the purple sky. The birds were chirping sleepily in the hedge above his head. He had not meant to sleep so long. Fanny's head was on his chest, and her curls were tickling his nose. Her body lay against his. He was strangely content. Nothing mattered any more except that he held Fanny in his arms. It was all very simple, he thought dreamily. I shall get us out of this predicament, and I shall marry her.

He sat up and raised Fanny up with him. She came awake, grumbling sleepily. He kissed her gently on the mouth. She tried to push him away, and then as if she, too, was feeling that same contentment, she relaxed against him and kissed him back.

They both sank back on the grass and lay there, kissing each other long and lazily. 'Marry me?' said the earl at last.

'How?' said Fanny. 'Mrs Waverley will not give her permission and was not responsible for our abduction.'

'Gretna,' he whispered against her lips. 'Why not?'

'Why not, indeed,' murmured Fanny, all thoughts of finding work as a governess vanishing as their lips joined in another long drugged kiss.

'Will we always quarrel?' she asked at last.

'Never again,' he said.

'Perhaps we should be on our way,' said Fanny. 'I think we should go to this village and throw ourselves on the mercy of the parish constable.'

'Of all the stupid ideas!'

'It is *not* stupid,' said Fanny, pushing him away. 'What's *your* famous idea?'

'We have a guinea. We find an inn and . . .'

'And get insulted and turned from the doors. Look at the mess we are in! A parish constable cannot think we are villains or we would not seek him out.'

'Listen to me . . . !'

'No! You listen to me, you overbearing, annoying creature,' raged Fanny. 'I come up with a perfectly sensible idea . . .'

'Which I accept,' he said, kissing her nose. 'I thought we weren't going to quarrel ever again.'

'You started it by being stupid and obnoxious and bullying.'

'Either you get up and on your way, Fanny,' he said, 'or I shall keep you here all night.'

The village proved to be a mile farther on. They were shown the roundhouse and soon confronted the parish constable, an elderly shopkeeper who had been regretting that it was his month to be constable and who brightened at this odd diversion. He believed the earl simply because he wanted to believe him. He was bored and tired, and the idea of having a real live earl in his roundhouse was surely something to tell his grandchildren. He accordingly sent a note to the local magistrate saying that he had the Earl of Tredair in the roundhouse, rather than saying he had someone claiming to be the Earl of Tredair.

The magistrate arrived and listened to the earl's story, appalled. Fanny had been right. The magistrate was perfectly sure an imposter would go nowhere near the authorities. He begged the earl to accept accommodation for the night at his own home, but the earl wearily asked the use of a carriage. The magistrate's servants could go to Brighton with them and make sure they were who they said they were.

The earl would have liked to enliven the journey by making love to Fanny, but the magistrate's wife had sent her own lady's maid to accompany Fanny and make all respectable. With a sinking heart, Fanny had heard the magistrate and his wife promising the earl that they would both swear the couple had been with them the whole time so that the earl should not be compromised.

It was five in the morning when the magistrate's

coachman knocked loudly on the knocker of the house in Brighton. At last Mrs Ricketts appeared, in cap and nightgown. She took one look at Fanny and the earl and began to cry with relief.

'Oh, Miss Fanny,' she sobbed. 'I knew you would not leave us without saying good-bye.'

Frederica and Felicity came hurtling down the stairs and into Fanny's outstretched arms. Then came Mrs Waverley, her heavy face alight with relief. Her stray chick was home. She had trounced Tredair before, and she could trounce him again.

As Fanny was led up the stairs by Felicity and Frederica after all the explanations, the earl said, 'A word with you, Mrs Waverley, after I have thanked these servants and sent them home.'

'Not tonight,' said Mrs Waverley. 'So much shock and worry have quite overset me. In the morning, my lord, I pray you.'

The earl nodded curtly and turned away.

Mrs Waverley began to plot and plan.

As Felicity and Frederica sat on the end of Fanny's bed after she had undressed, all came to the conclusion that Lady Artemis had played a trick on Fanny out of spite. 'They must be brought to court,' cried Felicity.

'No,' said Fanny. 'No scandal. I am going to marry Tredair and that will be scandal enough.'

'I do wish you would stop this silly business of marrying Tredair,' said Felicity. 'He doesn't want to marry you. He can't. He wants a mistress. He is only tricking you.'

'I am going to marry him with or without Mrs Waverley's permission,' said Fanny.

'Why?'

'I love him!'

'Nonsense,' said Frederica practically. 'You know you only think you are going to lead a free life by marrying him. But you won't have any freedom. You'll be his mistress, having bastard after bastard, like some sort of queen bee until he tires of you.'

'I am very tired already. Go away,' said Fanny furiously.

She was so angry with them, she thought she would not sleep, but her eyes began to close as soon as they had left the room.

ELEVEN

It was four the following afternoon before Mrs
Waverley agreed to see the earl.

Almost before he began to speak, he knew his
request to marry Fanny would be turned down.

Nonetheless, he began, 'I hope you will not continue to be foolish, Mrs Waverley. Fanny must be
allowed to marry me. You have no good reason to
stop her.'

'I have every reason,' said Mrs Waverley. 'Firstly,
I do not believe you. You promise marriage, but
you do not intend to go through with it. You want
Fanny as your mistress and do not like your will to be
crossed. Also, I think blaming your friend and Lady
Artemis for having abducted you a shabby thing to
do. It was you, my lord, who abducted Fanny. Is she
still a virgin?'

The earl's face darkened with fury. 'If you were

a man, I would strike you,' he raged. 'I am rapidly coming to the conclusion that you have a filthy mind!'

'I am a woman,' said Mrs Waverley, unmoved by his rage. 'Women have a natural modesty. Men do not. They wish to sate their lusts under the guise of a pretty name like love. Beasts, all!'

He looked at her fat, seemingly smug face and controlled himself with an obvious effort.

'Let me tell you this, Mrs Waverley, and listen well. I am leaving for London. I am going to wring Fordyce's neck and then begin arrangements to take Fanny away from you. Do not try to take her away from me or hide her. I shall return and find her wherever you have put her.'

Mrs Waverley crossed her hands in her lap and gave him a look like stone.

He gave her a brief bow and walked from the room. He went straight up to Fanny's bedchamber, thinking hard. He should not have put Mrs Waverley on her guard. The door opened before he could knock. 'I was waiting and listening for you,' said Fanny. 'What did she say?'

She stood aside to let him enter and then closed the door.

'She still insists on crediting me with the worst intentions. I want you to make sure she does not try to spirit you away, Fanny. So please pretend that you have dismissed me. No! You must listen. I must go to London and make preparations for our journey to Gretna. I must punch Fordyce's head, that is, if he is guilty, although it seems that way. I must wind up my affairs. Please go on as you would if you had not met me. Do not even confide in the other girls or in the servants. Do you understand?'

'She might see it in my eyes,' said Fanny. 'Hate, I mean. I do hate her for standing in my way.'

'Think only of pity when you look at her,' said the earl, trying to be reasonable, although at that moment he felt like throttling Mrs Waverley. 'She is a sad, frightened, lonely woman. In return for her previous kindness, treat her with courtesy until I come for you.'

'When will that be?' asked Fanny.

'A week. Look for me in a week's time.'

'We may not be here. She did not want to stay in Lady Artemis's house.'

'That, I think, was while Lady Artemis was in residence and likely to entertain. Now Lady Artemis has gone, and Mrs Waverley has her own servants and the three of you to herself. The news from London is that the mob did not get as far as Hanover Square. The militia stopped them in Oxford Street. But do not tell Mrs Waverley that. She may try to return to town, and I do not want to miss you when I come here and find you have set out for London.'

He held out his arms and Fanny went into them. He kissed her gently at first and then fiercely. 'Wait for me, Fanny, and trust in me,' he said urgently.

Lady Artemis and Mr Fordyce announced their betrothal in the newspapers. But they were not a very happy couple. Mr Fordyce was appalled at what he

199

had done, and Lady Artemis did not help by pointing out that members of society played worse jokes
on each other every day of the week. Mr Fordyce
envied her careless ways and easy conscience.

But Lady Artemis was disturbed. Sometimes she
wondered if she had really thought up that abduction
to help Fanny or whether it had been to punish Lord
Tredair for having given her a lecture. Mr Fordyce
always seemed to be in her home. She thought of
Mrs Waverley's words and felt her freedom eroding
away a bit at a time. Her servants now turned to Mr
Fordyce for their orders, not her. His perpetually
passionate and innovative lovemaking was beginning to make her feel like a slut. She had a longing
to be treated like a delicate flower, to be courted.
He had irritating little mannerisms that were rapidly beginning to grate on her nerves. She did not
like the way he made little slurping noises when he
drank his tea. She did not like the way he slapped
her on the bottom when lovemaking was over and
called her 'Good girl,' as if she were a horse that
had run well at Newmarket. She had canceled the
tutors after Mrs Waverley's lessons had begun. Now
she was anxious to resume her studies. All this had
happened in a mere two days.

Above all she missed the joys of the chase. What
was the point of going out to a ball or party when all
the gentlemen knew you were already someone else's
property.

By the third day she was beginning to hope Lord
Tredair *would* call Mr Fordyce out.

On the fourth day she learned that Tredair was already back in London. Why he had not come near her, she did not know, but she knew he would come soon. The fact that he was delaying his visit did not suggest a duel, rather it suggested an angry lord consulting his lawyers with a view to taking both of them to court.

That evening, Lady Artemis sent word to Mr Fordyce that she had a headache and he was on no account to call. She did not tell him the news of Tredair's return. Then she called her servants and asked them to get her traveling carriage ready and pack her bags. She was going to Paris. Peace had been declared, and the English were flocking to Paris for the first time in years.

At midnight, when the lights in Mr Fordyce's house across the square had been extinguished, Lady Fordyce made her way quietly into her traveling carriage. She sat on the edge of the seat, her hands clenched, waiting and waiting in case there should be a cry of alarm that would prove Mr Fordyce had seen her departure.

She sat bolt upright and rigid until a few miles had passed, and then she sank back against the upholstery and closed her eyes.

Freedom!

Perhaps on her return, she would seek out that odd woman, Mrs Waverley, and continue her studies.

The next day Mr Fordyce went eagerly across the square with a light step. He hammered on the door of Lady Artemis's house. Her butler opened it, but instead of immediately standing back to let Mr Fordyce enter, he barred the way.

'What is all this, Humphrey?' asked Mr Fordyce, surveying the butler's gloomy face. 'Mistress still ill?'

'The mistress has gone, sir,' said the butler.

'Gone out? Where? It is too early to make calls.'

'I mean, gone from London, sir.'

'Nonsense, Humphrey. I do not believe you.' Mr Fordyce pushed his way past and ran up the stairs. The drawing room was empty except for a footman in his shirt sleeves who was standing on a ladder shrouding the chandelier in holland cloth.

Mr Fordyce went up to Lady Artemis's bedchamber. It was a mess. Clothes were lying discarded everywhere, but he could tell after a glance that the best items in her wardrobe had gone.

'I told you so,' said the butler gloomily from the doorway. 'Here's a letter for you.'

'Why didn't you say so earlier, man?' said Mr Fordyce, seizing it and breaking open the seal.

'Dear Mr Fordyce,' he read, 'By the time you receive this, I shall be on my way to Wales to stay with a relative. Do not try to follow me. I made a great mistake and wish my freedom back again. I wish to terminate our engagement. Forgive me. A.V.'

'Where in Wales has she gone?' he cried. The butler, who knew very well his mistress was bound for Paris, shook his head. 'I do not know,' he lied. 'My lady would not tell us.'

Mr Fordyce was stricken. It dismally occurred to

him that Lady Artemis had never called him John. Even in moments of high passion. Why had she left? He had serviced her well. He had been tender and loving. He never so much as glanced at another woman. Why?

He made his way back to his own home and into his library and sat down and stared at the floor. He was still sitting staring at the floor an hour later when the Earl of Tredair was announced.

The earl had been wondering what to do about Mr Fordyce. He did not want to call him out. Duels had a nasty way of getting into the newspapers. Duels were now illegal, and he did not want to have to flee to the continent before his marriage. He could not take the matter to court without causing a scandal.

Mr Fordyce did not even look up as he came into the library.

'I find it hard to believe that you would play such a dirty trick,' said the earl, glaring down at him. 'It was you, wasn't it?'

'Yes,' said Mr Fordyce.

'Why, in God's name?'

'Lady Artemis wished you to be reconciled with Miss Fanny. She thought that might happen if she threw you together. Also, she thought you deserved to be cured of your high and mighty attitude as regards Miss Fanny's thieving.'

'Which you told her about after promising me not to breathe a word?'

Mr Fordyce shrugged. 'A man should have no

secrets from the woman he loves. We did it for the best. If you wish to challenge me to a duel, I am ready to meet you.'

He raised his eyes and the earl stifled an exclamation at the world of misery there.

'Where is Lady Artemis?' asked the earl.

'She is gone. She has left me. She wishes to cancel our engagement.'

'Why?'

'She says she wants to be free. Women were ever fickle. My heart is broken.'

'Hearts don't break,' said the earl cynically. Then he wondered how he would feel if he returned to Brighton and found Fanny did not want him. A cold feeling of dismay stole over him.

'I think you have been punished enough,' said the earl.

'Please tell me all is well with you and Miss Fanny?' pleaded Mr Fordyce.

The earl walked from the room without replying. He had no intention of confiding in Mr Fordyce again. He went home and rushed through the final arrangements for his departure. Was Fanny still missing him? Or had Mrs Waverley been seeping poison in her ears?

Fanny was finding it all a great strain. Frederica and Felicity were in high spirits. They loved Brighton. They were allowed to go out walking accompanied by Mrs Ricketts and were relishing their new freedom. Mrs Waverley was particularly tender to Fanny, stroking her hair at every opportunity, and calling her 'most beloved'.

Mrs Waverley had made a few friends among like-minded ladies of the town. In that way she was able to find out that all the gossip about her and the girls had died down. Only one piece of gossip had stuck and that was that all the Waverleys were fabulously rich. Tradesmen vied with each other for Mrs Waverley's custom and sent presents of wine and delicacies. Mrs Ricketts remarked to Fanny that when folks thought you were rich, you could live comfortably without spending a penny.

Fanny longed to confide in Frederica and Felicity but did not dare do so, apart from the fact she would be breaking her promise to the earl. The two girls appeared very young to Fanny now. They had reverted to their usual squabbles and horseplay.

They made Fanny tell the story of her abduction over and over again. They particularly liked the bits where the earl was taken for a villain.

Fanny said it was hard to understand, for the earl was handsome and did not have a sinister cast of face, but Frederica said his eyes were too clever. Proper gentlemen had blank, stupid eyes.

Lying in the bottom drawer of a bureau in her room were three letters Fanny had written. One was to Mrs Waverley and the other two to Felicity and Frederica. She planned to take them out and leave them on top of the bureau after she made her escape.

Soon the week of waiting was nearly over. Fanny

began to worry. What if he had forgotten about her in London? There were so many pretty women there, of good family too, who would be happy to have him for a husband.

She did not dare pack a trunk, but she went up to her room to sort out in her mind the clothes she would take with her. She planned to leave all her jewelry behind. She hated every bauble now.

She pushed open the door and let out a gasp. Frederica and Fanny were standing together at the window, reading those letters she had planned to leave behind when she eloped.

She ran forward and snatched them away, crying, 'How dare you poke and pry among my things!'

'I was looking for my pale pink shift,' said Frederica, hard-faced, 'and Mrs Ricketts said it might have been put with your things by mistake. What is the meaning of this, Fanny?'

Fanny looked at their furious faces and knew she was going to have to lie. If she pleaded with Frederica, if she told her of the elopement, then Frederica would be convinced the earl was tricking her and meant to make her his mistress.

'I wrote those some time ago,' said Fanny. 'I thought we were going to elope. But then I saw he could never marry me. I forgot about the letters. Tear them up. All is over between myself and the Earl of Tredair. I shall never see him again.'

The strain of the long week's wait told on Fanny at last, and she burst into tears, which was the best thing she could have done, for the two girls thought she was weeping because she had at last found out the earl's evil intentions.

Frederica and Felicity hugged her. Such had been Mrs Waverley's teaching that they both believed that no man would ever want them in marriage. Frederica vowed never to become as 'soft' as Fanny. She felt much older than Fanny and much harder. Any man would find it difficult to trick *her*.

'So I will take these nasty stupid letters away and burn them,' said Frederica. 'You are lucky we found them and not Mrs Waverley.'

That evening Fanny retired early after dinner. She sat down and wrote three more letters, wondering where to hide them this time.

There came a scratching at the door, and Fanny placed the letters under a large ewer on her toilet table and called, 'Come in!'

Mrs Ricketts entered and went quickly to Fanny's side. 'It's tonight, miss.'

'What is?' asked Fanny.

'The elopement, to be sure.'

Fanny clutched the housekeeper, her eyes shining. 'He has come back?'

'Yes, miss. I was out walking this afternoon when his servant approached me and gave me money and a letter. He knows there might be a terrible scene and the authorities called if he tries to take you out the front way. I cannot unlock the door for him, for I would lose my job.'

'So what is he going to do?'

'Come up to your bedchamber by a ladder in the

back garden. I've left the garden gate at the side of the house unlocked. I've brought a long rope. We have to lower your trunk into the garden first, as soon as it's dark.'

'Oh, Mrs Ricketts, bless you!'

'Don't bless me, miss, until you get clean away. Miss Felicity's likely to be lying awake reading, and her bedchamber overlooks the garden as well.'

'What time will he come?'

'Two in the morning. Now, for that trunk. Lock your door while I pack.'

Fanny brought out gowns and mantles, bonnets and pelisses while Mrs Ricketts arranged everything in a stout trunk. 'This will never do, miss,' she said straightening up. 'Your bonnets will get crushed in here. Hand me that bandbox from the top of the wardrobe.'

'I think we are taking too much,' said Fanny anxiously. 'Did he not say one trunk?'

'Well, his servants did. But men never think of practical things like what to do with bonnets.'

At last both trunk and bandbox were corded up. Mrs Ricketts tied them both firmly to a long length of rope while Fanny gently eased up the window. They heaved the luggage over the sill and began to lower it slowly.

'What if someone looks out and sees it?' hissed Fanny.

'Let's just hope they don't,' said Mrs Ricketts, 'and if they do, you're to swear blind it was all your own doing.'

There was a soft thud as bandbox and trunk hit the grass below.

'Now, it's up to you and my lord,' said Mrs Ricketts.

'You do not need to worry about your job here,' said Fanny, hugging the housekeeper. 'You can come to me.'

'I shall stay here, miss, and take care of the other two. Better for you to know they have someone looking out for their interests.'

After she had left, Fanny sat and waited. The hours at first dragged by and then seemed to speed up. Two o'clock came. Then ten past. Then half past.

Fanny was close to tears with the strain of waiting. What if he did not come?

And then she heard a grating sound from outside the window. She opened it again and leaned out. A ladder was propped against the sill. She turned about and took the letters from under the ewer and placed them on the mantelpiece.

The earl's face appeared at the window. 'Come,' he said softly.

'Do you really mean to marry me?' asked Fanny, suddenly afraid.

'Of all the stupid things to say,' he said crossly. 'I am not in the habit of climbing up ladders in the middle of the night to abduct females. Are you going to stand there twittering all night? I could shake you, Fanny.'

Fanny let out a nervous giggle and crossed to the window. 'Are you going to carry me over your shoulder?' she asked.

'No, Fanny, I think you are quite capable of getting down by yourself,' said the earl, beginning to back down the ladder.

Fanny climbed after him. The night was warm and the scents of the garden rose to meet her. When she reached the bottom of the ladder two servants glided out of the darkness and began to carry it away. The earl put a hand at her waist and hurried her through the garden.

The sound of the restless sea met their ears, and they climbed into a traveling carriage laden with luggage. There was another carriage behind with more luggage, and the earl's servants and four outriders carrying torches.

Fanny stood with one foot on the steps of the coach and looked up at the house.

Then she let out a gasp. Frederica was leaning out of a front window, her hair streaming about her shoulders.

Frederica saw the traveling coaches, the outriders, the earl, and Fanny.

'Come back, Fanny,' she screamed. 'He will betray you.'

The earl pushed Fanny into the carriage. 'Drive on,' he called to the coachman who whipped up the horses.

Frederica stayed there, clutching hold of the sill. What could she do? What could Mrs Waverley do? What could anyone in this whole household of women do? A stern father would have ridden after them, brothers would have challenged the earl to a duel, or magistrates would be called in to stop the marriage.

She turned away from the window. She did not go to Fanny's room. She knew now those letters had been written for this night. She went to Felicity's room. Felicity was lying awake, reading. She had just been reading about a most exciting elopement and so vivid had the description been that Felicity could have sworn she actually heard the ladder grate against the wall, the stifled whispers, and the carriages racing off into the night.

'Fanny's gone,' said Frederica. 'You must come with me to Mrs Waverley. I cannot bear her tantrums on my own.'

'Gone!' said Felicity. 'She has betrayed us.'

Frederica shrugged. 'In Fanny's case, she thinks it's the world well lost for love. She deserves our pity. She will learn her fate soon enough.'

'Those letters . . . ?'

'Yes, those were the letters we were supposed to find tomorrow morning. She has probably rewritten them. Let us collect them and go to Mrs Waverley.'

Mrs Waverley's rage was terrifying. She did not shout or weep as the girls expected her to, but sat like stone with only her pale eyes flashing fire.

'She will try to come back to us,' said Mrs Waverley, 'after he has ruined her. She is not to be allowed pity or charity.'

'Are women who fall from grace because of the machinations of some man not deserving of pity?' asked Frederica.

'No,' said Mrs Waverley. 'Not Fanny. You see what men are like? Stay with me. Keep close to me and all will be well.'

Despite her distress, Frederica saw a way of manipulating Mrs Waverley into allowing them more freedom.

'When you look at it,' she said, 'it is not entirely Fanny's fault.'

'How so?' asked Mrs Waverley.

'What do we know of men or the outside world? Had Fanny been allowed to go out more, she would not have fallen head over heels for the first man who looked at her. Now Felicity is in danger,' said Frederica, surreptitiously pinching Felicity's arm, a sign to that young lady to remain silent.

'Felicity?' cried Mrs Waverley. 'Has some man . . . ?'

'No,' said Frederica. 'But she has been addling her brains with romances from the circulating library.'

'She is not allowed to read romances!'

'There you are,' said Frederica. 'We are not allowed to do so many things that you must understand our lapses. If you continue to restrict our liberty, then we shall both, like Fanny, begin to see any man as the only means of escape.'

The angry fire died out of Mrs Waverley's eyes, and she began to look hunted. 'Leave me,' she said weakly. 'The shock of Fanny's betrayal has been great.'

The girls went back upstairs. 'Why did you have to tell her about me reading romances?' said Felicity fiercely. 'I thought we had given up telling tales on each other.'

'I had to frighten her,' said Frederica, 'else the shock of Fanny's escape should make her keep us housebound more than ever before.'

'Don't you think the earl means to marry Fanny?' asked Felicity. 'He went to an awful lot of trouble, and with his title and money he could get any woman he wanted.'

'They get jaded,' said Frederica, worldly wise. 'Women are like food to them. They are always searching out some new and different gourmet treat. If you think of poor Fanny at all, think of her lying naked on a platter with an orange in her mouth.'

Felicity began to giggle and Frederica to laugh. Mrs Ricketts heard the laughter and shook her head. It was all for the best. No one but herself had ever had one spark of affection for little Miss Fanny.

On their return to London, life certainly took a change for the better for the two remaining Waverley girls. Mrs Waverley took them out, not to balls and parties, but to plays and operas, museums and exhibitions, and occasionally for a drive in the Park. Instead of attiring them in their drab schoolgirl outfits, she compromised by dressing them in plain but fashionable clothes.

Frederica and Felicity often talked about Fanny. Frederica vowed that if she returned a broken reed in need of help, then they would help her every way they could. She never noticed that Felicity was always very silent on the subject of Fanny. Felicity had written a furious letter to Fanny to the earl's town house, calling her every name under the sun. She was already regretting that letter, but she had written it in the heat of the moment when she had felt betrayed by Fanny. Both girls believed that Mrs Waverley was right and that Tredair would ruin Fanny. That trust in Mrs Waverley's judgment bound the girls close to her.

Mrs Waverley was so delighted with the girls' new affection for her that she allowed Frederica one day to coerce her into taking them to the Park at the fashionable hour instead of driving out at a time when they could be guaranteed to meet as few people as possible.

The girls dressed in slightly finer clothes than they were usually allowed to wear. The day was chilly and gray. Both Frederica and Felicity prayed it would not rain, for they were to go to the Park in an open carriage.

The carriage was rented. Mrs Waverley would have loved a female coachman, but knew that would be far too shocking a thing for society to accept. So she always rented her carriages from the livery stables, which meant she did not have to tolerate menservants except on drives.

Frederica and Felicity were excited at the grand sight of all the fashionable clothes and glittering carriages. 'I think, girls,' said Mrs Waverley, leaning forward, 'that it is time I gave you an allowance. Pin money, you know.'

She leaned back smiling as the girls chorused their thanks. Mrs Waverley was happier than she had ever been before. She was loved by her girls. It was good that Fanny was gone. Fanny must have been the disruptive influence.

Then her face hardened. 'There is Mr Fordyce,' she said. 'Cut him!'

The girls turned their faces away, but Mr Fordyce rode along beside the carriage.

'Great news from Gretna!' he cried. 'Tredair and Fanny are married.'

Mrs Waverley's head jerked around to face him as if on wires. 'You must be mistaken. Stop!' she called to the coachman.

Mr Fordyce pulled a newspaper from a capacious pocket. 'It's in the evening paper,' he said. 'You may have it.' He dropped it on Mrs Waverley's lap and rode off.

'Is it true?' asked Frederica.

Mrs Waverley slowly read the account. There it all was. The Earl of Tredair and Miss Fanny Waverley were married at Gretna by the blacksmith over the anvil. The earl was quoted as saying he would marry his countess again in church as soon as she reached her majority.

Frederica snatched the paper from Mrs Waverley and Felicity, and she read it with their heads together.

A witness at the wedding was quoted as saying he had never seen a couple so much in love.

Frederica felt betrayed, not by Fanny, but by Mrs Waverley.

'Move on,' cried Mrs Waverley to the coachman. She avoided the girls' eyes.

'Got to stay where we are for a bit, madam,' called the coachman. 'Seems His Royal Highness is approaching.'

'Drive on! I command you!' cried Mrs Waverley, turning quite white.

'Can't do that, madam,' said the coachman. 'Everyone stops for the prince.'

All the carriages were lined up. A swan-necked phaeton, driven by the Prince Regent himself, came bowling slowly along, the prince nodding and waving to first one and then the other.

He came alongside the Waverleys' carriage. It all happened so quickly, but Frederica saw the startled and then half-ashamed look in the prince's eyes as he stared at Mrs Waverley. Mrs Waverley was ashen-faced.

'Good day to you,' said the prince and drove quickly away.

'I did not know you knew the Prince Regent,' cried Frederica.

'I don't,' said Mrs Waverley. 'I met him briefly at Lady Artemis's salon, that is all. Oh, please move, driver, and take us home.'

Frederica clutched the newspaper, her mind in a whirl. She had often wondered who exactly Mrs Waverley was and where she came from. By the time they reached home, she was determined to find out. There was a mystery here, and solving that mystery might give her a hold over Mrs Waverley, a hold that would mean more freedom and independence.

'And where do we go now?' asked Fanny, after that first delirious night of lovemaking as man and wife. 'Do we go back to London?'

'No, I have decided we are to go to France on our honeymoon,' said the earl.

They were in his carriage, moving down the Great North Road. Fanny leaned her head against his chest and sighed, 'I would like to see Frederica and Felicity again.'

'And so you shall, my sweet, after our honeymoon. That will give them time to forgive you.'

'I cannot yet get used to being so free and happy,' said Fanny.

'Don't you feel tied to me?'

'Yes, but not imprisoned. I am still a modern woman and demand my rights, my lord. Kiss me!'

He folded her in his arms and kissed her passionately while the coach lurched and swayed down the long road south.